The Lost Scroll

SERENUS

The Lost Scroll

SERENUS

Tahira Ejaz & Khalid Ejaz

FACT & *Lore*
PUBLISHING INC

All rights reserved. Published by Fact and Lore Publishing Inc.

ISBN 978-1-7781900-1-8 (paperback)
ISBN 978-1-7781900-2-5 (hardcover)
ISBN 978-1-7781900-0-1 (ebook)

For my amazing children.

Contents

Part III

Loading 'Serenus_beta_version_DO_NOT_USE_contains_bugs'...

Chapter 1

In my dream, I heard a voice:

"Your vessel is sinking; survive the tides.

The end is coming; open your eyes."

The voice kept repeating like an alarm. I heard it but did not wake up. Then, a much louder sound startled me, and my eyes shot open. I listened to the splashing of waves, but that was not what had woken me. The startling sound was gone.

I tried to sit up but lost my balance. My hand stretched out instinctively and held on to something for support. I couldn't see anything. It was too bright, and my vision was blurry.

Another splash turned my attention to my surroundings, and I found myself on a small boat. There were waves all around me, rocking me back and forth and left and right. I grabbed the other side to balance myself.

The water stretched as far as I could see, and the furious waves battered my small, powerless boat, making it wobble dangerously.

I sat with fearful eyes and a straight back and tightened my grip on both sides. The wind whipped my face as I listened to the splattering of the boat rising and falling on the tides. My eyes darted from right to left, back to the right, at my arms, and my tense legs spread in front. My body was trying to adjust itself to get in sync with the movement of the water, tightening my muscles here, relaxing there, struggling for balance against the continuous pounding.

I felt small, very small, an insignificant object in the vast and immense body of water around me. I was hanging on for dear life with the only goal of staying upright. Feeling helpless and terrified, I was giving in to the crippling fear in one moment, fighting it back in the next.

A loud growl vibrated through the air. I turned my head around and saw an island I had just passed. With wide eyes, I recognized an Albertosaurus. And behind it, a very long-necked Brontosaurus reaching for the tallest treetops. In the background were the Rocky Mountains with snow-covered peaks. The sight of the incredible giants excited me. I was being carried farther and farther away, but I kept looking back till they disappeared out of sight.

Then I remembered the warning in my dream. The voice was alerting me to the sinking of a vessel. Did it mean my boat? I panicked and checked for leaks. Fortunately, it didn't show any signs of collapsing. There was no water inside, and the side walls were high enough to shield me from the splashing waves. The voice in the dream was wrong. My boat was not sinking.

That was when I found the watch on my wrist. A very strange watch, as it didn't tell time. Instead, it showed downward spiraling water. Being in the water and seeing a whirlpool on my wrist made me more anxious. I looked around, but as far as I could tell, there was no vortex in sight.

The thought of a whirlpool had scared me. With growing panic, I tried to remember if I knew how to swim but immediately realized that I couldn't possibly escape it even if I could.

I sat up to see farther away. But the moment I did, the boat started to rock dangerously. I quickly lowered myself and spread out my arms to find balance.

For some time, the boat moved on, and I looked around helplessly. Then, far ahead of me, I spotted an island. A sigh of relief left my lungs, and my muscles relaxed. The land was still far away, and I had no means to change direction, but that was alright—I was headed straight toward it.

The possibility of reaching the ground made me feel a bit better, but the thought of dinosaurs worried me. Even if I reached the island and survived the water, how would I survive the land?

I looked behind but found no land where I could have come from. I wondered why I was in the boat. I had no memory of getting in it. In fact, now that I thought of it, it shocked me that I had no memories at all.

I searched myself and found nothing but a piece of paper in my pocket. I held it in one hand, and read the words:

Your vessel is sinking; survive the tides,

The end is coming; open your eyes.

Live and think, but don't you stall,

Catch the wizard, go past the fall.

The prophecy is cruel and very clever,

The fruitless war goes on forever,

Look to the future, but first in your past;

Know that your world is oh so vast!

I turned the paper over. There was nothing on the other side.

Strange! I had heard the poem in my dream and then found it on a piece of paper in my pocket.

I was still quite scared, but the poem had distracted me. To keep my thoughts from drifting back to the whirlpool, or the absence of any memories of the past, I read the poem over and over again.

I was now very close to the island, heading straight to the middle, where the water divided the land into two halves. A huge green forest covered most of the ground, except for a darker patch that looked like it was burnt down. Soon, there was land on both sides of the boat, and the waterway shrank till it was only a few feet wide.

I wanted to stop, but the banks were rocky, so I waited for a better place. The current was much faster now. Or so it felt.

In the distance were some wooden houses. I couldn't believe my luck. Someone was living on this island. As I got closer, I saw a group of people who had spotted me as well. They waited for me to reach them and then started to run alongside the boat. And as they were running, they were singing:

"Your vessel is sinking; survive the tides,

The end is coming; open your eyes."

I sat helplessly and watched them with a mix of fear and confusion. They kept running along, repeating the rhyme over and over again like a warning. I became very anxious and couldn't wait to get out of the boat.

I had now reached a part of the shore with no rocks. Further ahead, I heard—and then saw—a waterfall with a misty fog surrounding it. Large stones blocked access to the fall, but water pushed around the narrow gaps and fell to the depths below. The path was not wide enough for a boat to pass through. Still, I had to stop quickly to avoid smashing into the rocks.

In a panic, I paddled with both hands and changed the direction just enough to go over the shallow sandy area. It slowed the boat considerably, but the fast current threatened to topple it.

When I felt safe enough, I jumped out, and some people ran to help me drag my boat out of the water.

I fell down on my knees and breathed a sigh of relief. Finally, I was out of danger.

The people watched me intently. They had lean figures with delicate-looking wings protruding from their backs, which shimmered softly as the sunlight reflected off them. Just as they fluttered their wings lightly, my back muscles moved too, and something moved behind me, making the same fluttering sound. In a surprise, I turned my head to look over my shoulder and discovered that I, too, had wings.

I stretched my wings in awe when one of the people came forward, put her hand on my shoulder, and said in a gentle, comforting voice, "You are safe now." She had the same watch on her wrist. I glanced at the others—they were all wearing one.

A loud whistle rang through the air, making everyone step away from me. A group of armed men and women tore through the forest. They charged with such speed that they surrounded me without giving me a chance to react. All I could do was stand up, looking at them helplessly.

They wore thin armor and held their spears pointed at me. Large bows hung over their shoulders, right next to their wings. They were older than the boys and girls I had just met. Their bodies had the same stature, but their wise faces revealed their mature age.

For a while, they just stood there, surrounding me. I waited. They said nothing. I looked around, wondering what was going on. They stared back at me, still doing nothing. The only sound came from the waterfall that ran noisily, completely ignoring the awkward silence around it.

Finally, the sound of running footsteps broke the baffling silence, and a girl ran from the forest with a notebook in her hand. As soon as she arrived, one of the guardians stepped forward and ordered, "Come with me." He started walking toward the falls.

Others waited for me to move. I looked at their spears and decided it was best to obey. Walking behind them, the girl with the notebook was constantly observing me.

I began to panic as we moved forward. Why were they taking me to the falls? Would they push me off the ledge? Why had they surrounded me? Their spears and bows hinted at the possibility of their being violent. I gathered some courage and asked them, but they wouldn't answer. We were now very close to the edge. The water ran fast between the moss-ridden rocks, and I was hesitant to go any farther.

The one in front went closer to the edge and turned to a muddy path. I followed, relieved that they were not going to throw me over.

The path led us down one side of the fall. Under it was an island surrounded by the rushing water that fell around it. A movable bridge was the only way to reach the island.

A man moved the bridge, went over, and ordered me to follow him. I walked across, looking at the large tree that covered most of the tiny piece of land.

The tree stood like a giant umbrella, except the sides came down to the ground, creating a hollow space underneath it. Long tresses of light blue flowers made the walls.

The armored man pulled back the floral curtain to reveal a dimly-lit chamber under the tree. He asked me to go inside, and as I walked in, he closed the opening behind me and left, leaving me alone.

The tree trunk stood like a pillar in the center. The thick branches arched up and outwards and fell back to the ground as thin, hanging vines. I peeked through the natural walls to see what was happening outside. The man was leaving through the bridge. Once he reached across, the bridge was moved away. I was left alone on the island. It felt like they had put me in prison.

When I was sure there was no one around, I walked out of the tree and glanced at the surroundings. The current around the tiny island was scary enough to keep me from trying to escape, but on one side, the stream was so narrow that I could easily jump across and head to the dense forest.

The waterfall was loud, and no other sound could be heard. I checked the top of the falls and didn't find anyone observing me. I wondered why they would leave me in a prison that I could easily escape from. Would something happen if I tried to run?

I walked to the narrower crossing, frequently checking the top of the fall to make sure no one was watching, then jumped across the stream.

With my head held low under the shade of my hands, I ran to hide in the nearest bushes. My wings spread out behind me like a shield. I had expected a hail of arrows or spears to attack me, but nothing happened. I was utterly puzzled. I peeked out of my hiding place but found no one watching me escape. This made no sense.

I tried to stretch my wings to see if I could fly away, but they were too delicate to trust with flight. None of the people I had met had actually used their wings to fly—I had only seen them walk.

After thinking for a while, I decided to go back and stay in *prison*. I wanted to know what it was all about. I also did not want to go into the forest for fear of encountering any dinosaurs. Being with people felt like a safer choice.

I walked back to the tree chamber slowly, constantly glancing up to the top of the waterfall, trying to understand their mysterious measure of bringing me to the island under the fall.

Once inside, I sat down against the tree and waited. I looked at my watch. Even though I was out of water, it still showed the whirlpool.

A scraping sound alerted me. The bridge was being moved again, and someone walked across it. Judging by the faint footsteps on the bridge, I guessed it was more than one person. I stayed where I was, alert and ready to expect the unexpected.

As their footsteps approached closer, two pairs of hands moved the vines aside, and three people entered my tree prison cautiously. The two on the side were heavily armored. I stood up and waited in anticipation. Their armor had an assortment of strange-looking markings, making them look higher in rank than the men and women who had surrounded me earlier.

Standing between the two armored men was a lady with no

armor. Her eyes squinted in concentration as she walked toward me and introduced herself. "I am Feray, and these are my guardians. Do you have powers? Magic, to be precise?"

"No! No, I don't have powers," I mumbled. "Magical powers, to be precise."

"Is that true? I will find out in no time." She sounded proud.

She called someone named Boris to come inside. As he came in, I saw more people outside the tree. The girl with the notebook was there too.

Boris carried a glass vial the size of a melon. Its whitish contents glowed softly inside. He placed it in front of me and asked me to sit down. I obeyed, observing the vial cautiously.

The lady ordered me to put my hands on the vial. I was nervous. It looked innocent, but I had just heard her ask about magic. I couldn't take it lightly. I didn't know what was going to happen. When I hesitated to touch the vial, the guardians moved closer, their weapons pointed at me. The lady looked at me with a piercing stare and knitted eyebrows and ordered, "Go on!"

Reluctantly, I obeyed and placed my hands on the glowing orb. It was cool and smooth to the touch. Its glow engulfed my hands. I closed my eyes and waited for something to happen. The vial stayed still and quiet. I peeked from behind my eyelids and saw the dim, whitish contents change into a greenish-white color. I looked at the lady to see what it meant. Her taut expression had changed, and she appeared relaxed now. She took the vial from my hands. With her, the glow turned white and blindingly bright. She returned the vial to Boris, who left with it.

The guardians relaxed and drew back their spears, bringing them back to their side.

Feray spoke softly this time, "Newcomer! You were right. You have no magic. Welcome to Serenus!"

It was a welcome change in her tone, but I couldn't help but feel a little disappointed at not having magic.

The guardians took a step back and moved the flowery tresses aside. Feray walked out through the opening. They kept the vines separated like an open curtain and looked at me. I stood up and followed Feray, watching the changed expression on their faces. To my surprise, they were smiling. Would they be smiling if I had magic? Maybe not. Lucky escape.

Outside the tree, a man stood waiting. He had an air of wisdom and confidence about him. He introduced himself, "I am Kratos. Feray was testing to see if you have any magical abilities. I apologize, but this is necessary."

He paused. I didn't say anything; instead, I studied him closely. He was a tall and muscular man. His broad shoulders and big arms made him stand out. His long, black, curly hair was tied up neatly. When he spoke, his voice was deep and gentle, "Welcome to Serenus! As long as you live in peace, this place will be your home."

My home? I repeated his words in my head. There was so much I wanted to ask. Where was I? Who were they? Why was I here? But for the moment, I decided to stay quiet and see what would happen next. Earlier, they were treating me like an enemy, but now things appeared to be heading in the right direction. I did not want to say anything to upset them. Although, I did feel more confident now.

Kratos asked me to follow him. We left the small island through the bridge and headed back up to the falls.

Once atop the fall, we trekked a path toward the forest. Around us, the grass was a fresh green, and countless wildflowers decorated it beautifully. The trees were laden with leaves as varied, as vibrant, and as beautiful as the flowers underneath. The more I saw, the more beautiful I found this place.

Feray stayed quiet and walked ahead of us. Kratos and I were side-by-side. The armed guardians had disappeared on a different path. The girl with the notebook still followed us quietly.

Kratos told me about the island. It was called Serenus, the land of peace. The inhabitants were Seren, and they had lived here for as long as they could remember. Every one of them had arrived on the island in the same way: in a boat. He had come decades ago and worked as a blacksmith.

Feray volunteered no information. She walked on, keeping to herself. Kratos kept glancing at her uneasily, seemingly anxious by her silence.

Suddenly, Kratos pointed ahead and announced, "Our village!"

The first thing I saw was a cluster of surprisingly wide trees full of colorful flowers that glowed brightly in the sun. The trees were unlike all the other trees in the forest. These were not too tall, maybe twice as tall as me, but were unusually wide. Tresses loaded with flowers hung down the sides just like the tree on the island under the fall. Each tree had flowers of a different color and stood in a circle around a much larger white-flowered tree.

Kratos pointed to a wooden house nearby. "Feray lives here."

We turned right and came upon a big village of wooden homes with beautiful front gardens. We continued on the path to a large clearing with a banquet area in the middle. Many men and women sat around these tables, enjoying the food as they chatted merrily. It was a very festive environment. I had already loved the beauty of the place, and now it looked even more inviting.

Kratos guided me to a table filled with food. Everyone's eyes were on me. An older woman stood up slowly and greeted me silently with the raise of a drink and a slow nod. Others bowed their heads with her. I mirrored the gesture. She sat down, all eyes turned away from me, and the Seren became busy in their own conversations.

Kratos introduced me to the girl with the notebook. Her name was Aymelek, and she was Feray's apprentice. As I sat next to her, she greeted me kindly and offered me a platter full of food.

I chose some delicious-looking apricots and ripe peach. A man brought soup for us. Following Aymelek's lead, I tasted the sweet, tangy soup. It was appetizing but gave no hint of its ingredients.

Feray told me that this was the midday meal. Everyone ate this meal in the village center. She clarified that we could eat wherever we wanted, but most people chose to eat there. I had a feeling she preferred it that way. It felt like an instruction I was supposed to follow.

Kratos and Feray left after they finished eating. Aymelek stayed as I ate slowly, looking around at the beautiful place I had found myself in. She spoke nicely, "You will stay at the Serenus Lodge until your home is ready."

I nodded, surprised to know that I would get a home here. It was all very mysterious; I didn't know where I had come from and why. And why were these people being so friendly to me, feeding me excellent tasting food, and they were even going to give me a home to live in. I was impressed by how kind everyone was. Except for Feray, I reminded myself. She did not feel very welcoming, although her words were not harsh.

After the food, Aymelek walked me to my temporary residence: a room in the Serenus lodge. I had so many questions that demanded answers, but she told me that she had a lot of work to finish before dark. But before she left, she said, "I understand how you feel. Every newcomer has questions. I promise I will provide answers in the morning. Until then, please stay in your room."

It was only a little after midday, and I had to wait for the following day to get more answers. I understood that they had other things to do, but it would've been better if they had allowed me to explore my new world on my own. Once again, I had the feeling of being in prison.

I looked around the room and found a note on the bedside table. In big, bold letters, it read:

Welcome to Serenus! What's your name?

And at the bottom,

Please do not roam around at night.

And then there was a sign that looked like a small dinosaur. I thought this card could have been an excellent place for some text to introduce me to this world, but there was nothing else on it.

I did not know my name. Why not? How did I lose my memories? Maybe Aymelek could answer that in the morning. Kratos said everyone came in a boat. They might know where they came from.

I tried to remember my past, but there was no memory. I spent a few moments thinking of a name that I could use temporarily till I remembered who I was, but it felt meaningless. I had to remember who I truly was. I sat with my head between my knees, focusing on finding any memory of why I got into a boat. What convinced me to venture out in the water in a tiny boat, and why? Was I running from something? Did someone make me leave by force? Nothing, absolutely nothing, came to mind.

As was expected of me, I stayed inside the room for the rest of the day and spent most of the time looking through the window. I could see a small section of a stone pathway. Occasionally, someone would appear on the path, and I would start watching them intently till they disappeared out of my view. People were busy in their routine lives. They looked comfortable and at ease. Maybe this was a safe place. These people could have behaved in any way, but they were nice to me. I comforted myself with the thought that wherever I had come from, this wasn't such a bad place to be. It could have been a lot worse.

Eventually, I got bored of looking at the same thing outside the window and started pacing around. Then, I stood in the middle of the room and spread my wings. I wished to be outside and have the freedom to test my wings, but, for now, bound by the walls around me, I could only stretch.

A knock at the door startled me. It was a kind man who brought my dinner and left with a smile. His smile made me feel better - and safer. A smile from a person I had never met before comforted me. How amazing was that? He smiled, something changed inside my head, and I felt better. Magical!

Of course, I understood that I was reading their gestures to judge their intentions. And they were giving me no reason to be scared. Yet, I was not done making up my mind. The people seemed nice, which was a great start, but I needed more. Everything was new and strange, and that made me feel unsure.

After observing the effects of a smile on my mental state for a bit longer, I reminded myself that this was a normal thing and did not warrant this much thinking. I shook my head to move away from the thought.

Magic… Did people here have magical abilities? I didn't. What could they do? So far, I hadn't seen anything that felt unusual except for the vial that changed color when I touched it. When Feray held the vial, it became much brighter. Did she have magic? I felt a little scared of her and pushed the thought out of my head.

I went to bed, still very confused and not fully believing the things I had experienced. I dreamed of a sinking vessel, a dangerous whirlpool, and a smiling Albertosaurus. And best of all, I dreamed of flying high above the clouds and over the Rocky Mountains, watching the majestic dinosaurs roam underneath.

Chapter 2

When I answered the knock at my door the following day, I found a cheery-looking Aymelek standing there. She had brought breakfast along with her notebook and informed me that we would stay in for a while, she would answer my questions, and then we could go out.

I found her taking notes frequently. She looked around my room and noted something, then looked at the open window and made a checkmark. I figured it was just part of her job, so I didn't question it.

She started the conversation by asking me if I slept well, then talked about her job. She was Feray's apprentice, but it was also her duty to introduce the newcomers to life on the island.

We walked to the window, where two chairs were placed next to a table. Aymelek waited for me to pick a seat. I sat on the chair with a view of the outside. Again, she wrote something, placed the breakfast basket on the table, and took the other chair. I watched her closely for the first time.

She did not appear much older than me and was quite thin, with long brown hair tied up in an intricately designed bun. Various rings lined her fingers. She must love leaves, as every ring had leaves in its design except one, a simple ring with a large, white translucent sphere. But it was no ordinary ring. Inside it, wisps of white swirled around slowly. I wondered what could be in there. It looked magical. I noticed her turning it around her finger frequently.

She smiled and asked, "What do you want to start with? Answers or breakfast?"

I replied quickly, "Answers, please."

"Okay. First of all, there are no dinosaurs on the island. We have found some fossils, but never an alive dinosaur."

I breathed a sigh of relief but then felt disappointed. As scary as the dinosaurs were, it would have been incredible to see and live among them.

"Relieved and disappointed is how every newcomer feels after hearing this." She laughed.

Before I could ask a question, she said, "Every one of us has come to this island just like you did. We heard the warning of a sinking vessel in our dream. Then we woke up to the sound of an Albertosaurus. We found ourselves in a boat and were terrified of a nonexistent whirlpool. Just like you must have been. Then we found a strange poem in our pocket, a mysterious watch on our wrist, and no memories of our past."

She paused. Her words were unbelievable. Every single person had come here in the exact same way as I did. But from where and why?

Aymelek adjusted her big, white ring and continued, "We have all wondered about our wings and found that the best they can do is carry us over a short distance. We can't fly high up in the sky. Am I right so far? Has that been your experience?"

I nodded, and she put a checkmark in her notebook.

Once again, I had just opened my mouth to ask my next question, but she answered it without even hearing it.

"No one has stopped at the dinosaur island on their way here. We all woke up only after it was too late to go there. We turned our heads back and watched it disappear behind us as the current carried us forward. Tell me, how amazing were the Rocky Mountains?"

I remembered the scene in my head and replied, "So amazing. So magnificent."

Aymelek slid her notebook toward me and, with her finger, pointed at the text in her notebook.

So amazing. So magnificent.

I read it and looked at her in wonder. How did she know I would say this?

She continued with a smile, "I have met many newcomers, and in the beginning, everyone asks the same questions. And when asked about the Rocky Mountains, everyone answers using the exact same words. We don't know why, but everyone answers this question like this."

This was so weird. Disappointment weighed on me. With every answer, it was becoming apparent that I was quite ordinary. There was nothing special about me. But, it also showed that we were all connected in some way.

Unaware of my thoughts, she went on, "Some people believe that the poem is a guide. We are supposed to do things the way they have been told in the poem. They believe it is our mission. But a vast majority believe that it is not like that. There is no mission, and we aren't supposed to walk a predetermined path. After all, the poem is wrong. No vessel has ever sunk. People arrive here, live their lives, grow old, and then die. But yes, it is very mysterious that we start with the poem."

I looked outside the window and thought about what she had just said. I was not convinced that the poem lacked any deeper meaning.

As I looked back at her, she continued, "Over time, we have learned that the best way to live here is by being kind, generous, and accommodating. All of us contribute to this world and, in return, benefit from it. I am an apprentice with Feray, a healer who works with the magical trees. Kratos is a blacksmith. All of us do our part in one way or another. You will be expected to do the same. Every newcomer gets a place on the island. It is their home for as long as they live in peace. We have devised a very fair system to allot land to newcomers. Each next arriver gets the next available plot going away from the village center."

After she put another checkmark in her notebook, she offered, "Now ask me any questions you want, and I will answer as well as I can. But before that, tell me—have you picked a name for yourself? Many newcomers pick a name right away, while some wait to decide later on."

She waited patiently as I processed the information. I wasn't interested in a name. All I wanted was more answers. "Where do we come from?"

Once again, she checked something in the notebook and then gave a short and straightforward answer: "No one knows!"

"Why did we come here?"

She made yet another checkmark in her notebook, raised her shoulders, and shook her head. "We don't know that either."

"Has anyone ever tried to go back and find out?" It bothered me that they did not know these answers. I thought these were the most straightforward and obvious questions. If they had lived here for so long, why didn't they find out?

"Many have tried, but no one has succeeded in going back as much as a single step. The current is too strong to travel against it, but it's not just the water; there is more to it. We cannot even throw a rock back in that direction. There is an invisible barrier that stops anything from going that way. We can move freely on this island, though."

I sat back in the chair and rubbed my head, trying to understand everything she had said. It was too much to take in so quickly.

"I know it's a head spinner," she added, "but in a little while, you will get used to it, and then it won't feel so strange anymore."

"If we can't go back, how about going forward?"

"Yes, we have tried that as well. And we've found that we can go forward. But no one who left has ever come back. The principle stays the same: we can only go in the direction of the current, and it never changes its direction. It never slows down or speeds up. If someone leaves the island, they leave it forever. Therefore, we don't know what lies beyond, or if there is anything there at all."

"That is so strange!" I exclaimed. Every answer brought more questions.

She nodded. "We have looked from the highest places on the island but didn't find any other piece of land around ours. All we can see is a dark curtain that blocks all probing. Those who leave, leave prepared to die, accepting that there is no coming back and that there might not be another island to stop at."

"But if there is the dinosaur island and then this one, there could be more ahead. I think it is quite possible, don't you?"

She shifted uncomfortably in her chair. For a moment, she stayed quiet and focused on her rings. Then, with a sigh, she looked up and forced a smile, "You are right, it is possible, but we can't know for sure. And there was no black curtain blocking our view as we traveled from the dinosaur island to this one. But there is one ahead of us. So, things could be different." A sad look took over her face. "We send our dead forward in their boats with gifts and flowers, hoping that they will reach a better place. Everyone arrives in a boat, and unless there is an accident, leaves in a boat. And so, we keep our boats with us for our entire life. This island is our home, and Serenus is our world."

It was a grim topic, but judging by her low tone, I felt that her sadness had another reason. I asked gently, "Aymelek, did you lose someone?"

She nodded without any expression on her face.

I put my hand on hers to comfort her. "I'm so sorry, Aymelek."

She forced a smile. "Thanks. It happened a few weeks ago. I'm sorry if I made you sad. Don't let it dampen your spirits. Our world is so beautiful, and there is so much that will amaze you." She paused for a bit and then continued, "It is important to understand how to live here, and once you learn the basics, it can be a lot of fun." Then she pointed toward the breakfast. "Let's eat now. We can continue our conversation later."

We ate in silence. I kept going over all the strange answers I had received and the new questions they brought.

After breakfast, she wrote a few more things in her note-book. I was very self-conscious because of her studying eyes and constant note-taking, wondering what she might be writing and whether I was behaving as expected, so I decided to ask her about it.

Before she could respond, a small Albertosaurus appeared outside the window. For a moment, it startled me, but then I realized that it was a flat piece of wood that was cut and painted to look like a dinosaur head. Suddenly, a thought flashed in my mind. What If the dinosaur I saw while coming to the island was also a fake? What if everything that she told me was a trick? The disturbing thought took over my mind for a fraction of a second, but I suppressed my expressions to hide what I was thinking.

Aymelek shifted the subject from the island to her notebook. She held it up and said, "This is a part of my job. I'm supposed to observe every newcomer and analyze their personalities. I'm glad you asked because it is important to understand. In the beginning, almost everyone who arrives here behaves in the same way and has the same questions, but, deep down, we are a little different from each other, and soon after our initial experiences, our small differences send us on very unique paths. We start looking at things in our own way."

She found me listening intently and continued, "For instance, when I came in, I noticed that the window was open. Yesterday, you escaped the island under the waterfall but then came back voluntarily—instead of running away, you wanted to know what was going on. Instead of focusing on choosing a name, you focused your attention on getting answers to your questions. And then your questions about going back and forward confirmed that you have an exploratory mind."

She was right. I was still exploring many options in my head, wondering about different possibilities, and one of those was that everything that she was telling me was a trick.

I nodded. She continued with a smile, "When I became sad, you felt my pain and tried to console me. This tells me that you are sensitive and empathetic, and your first instinct was to somehow make me feel better."

I smiled back, happy that she had felt my care. She went on, "We do our part by giving a good welcome. The first experiences in the life of a newcomer are the most impactful, and we try to do the best we can. Good experiences make good people, and it is easier to be nice today than to deal with a dangerous person later on."

She glanced at her notebook and added, "Please understand that I am not judging you. My goal is not to decide whether you did something in the right or wrong way. For example, you were awake and ready to meet me when I arrived. Instead, you could have been sleeping, and many people are, and that's perfectly alright. It is a lot to take in, so many people have trouble falling asleep for the first few nights, and that's why they wake up later in the morning. This analysis is just a starting point, and nothing we learn at this stage is certain. Over time, you will find what interests you, which will shape your life's direction. This personality analysis also helps us to give you the right job, the one that matches your interests."

I was very impressed to hear about their arrangement regarding land allotment, providing good experiences, personality assessment, and work assignments. But the presence of an invisible barrier around the island was hard to believe.

Then I recalled how guardians had surrounded me upon my arrival. They had threatened me with their spears and put me in prison under the waterfall, then they tested me to see if I had magic. That was definitely not a good experience. It wasn't friendly or welcoming at all.

I asked, "Why was I tested for magic?"

Aymelek responded casually, "Each one of us is different from others, and very rarely, someone arrives with abilities that we can not explain. Anything we cannot understand is considered a magical ability, and people with magic need a different starting environment and orientation."

"What kind of abilities do people have?"

"Feray can work with light. I can, too, though I am still learning to control it better. Another person here can feel what others are feeling."

Aymelek paused as someone knocked at the door. She carried her notebook with her, opened the door, and handed it to someone outside. Then she turned around and asked, "Do you want to ask more questions?"

I had received enough information to process. It overwhelmed me. Before I could answer, Aymelek opened the door just a little, peeked outside, then looked back at me, smiled, and said, "Whenever you have a question, you can come to me. Let's go out now."

I was happy to hear that. I wanted to go out and see the world. I got up quickly and followed Aymelek out of the door.

The moment I stepped outside, I found the entire village gathered there. Everyone screamed, "Surprise!" followed by many cheers, whistles, and horns. A rhythmic drum beat filled the air. It startled me at first, but I recovered quickly.

With wide eyes and a puzzled smile, I watched as they split into two groups, leaving a path in the middle that led to the village center. Aymelek and I walked toward it as the crowd cheered and danced on both sides.

It was hard to contain the excitement that filled my heart with their generous hospitality, and I thanked everyone. A seating area had been set up in front of a makeshift stage. Aymelek brought me to the front row. Behind us, the Seren started taking seats.

I couldn't believe what was happening. It felt incredible. If I were asked to describe my feelings at the moment, I wouldn't be able to find the words. I understood that they were going above and beyond, trying to give me the best early experiences that I could have. It would only be right to pay it back in as many ways as possible.

As I sat down, I asked Aymelek when they prepared for this. "Yesterday evening and today when we were chatting inside." The answer came with a big smile.

I looked at everyone behind me, thanking them happily with a smile and a nod.

The music stopped, and a loud voice from the stage stole my attention.

"Welcome, people of Serenus and our newest comer!"

A massive roar from the crowd followed. Goosebumps of excitement rose on my skin.

After the noise receded, the person on the stage continued, "Welcome…." He glanced at Aymelek's notebook and resumed, "Welcome, newcomer! We are delighted to have you. On be-half of the entire village, I welcome you to Serenus, the land of peace. We hope you will live a happy and healthy life."

He paused for a moment as the crowd clapped.

Then he continued, "And ladies and gentlemen, our drama club is ready to entertain you with their outstanding performance. Please enjoy!"

Loud cheering and clapping followed his announcement and continued for some time but then quieted down to a sudden hush as the music started again.

Many boys and girls ran onto the stage from one side. They were holding boards with waves painted on them. Two girls arrived carrying a boat from both ends, rocking it on the waves, with a boy pretending to be sitting in the boat, asleep.

The ones carrying the waves started chanting:

"Your vessel is sinking; survive the tides.

The end is coming; open your eyes."

The sleeper in the boat moved but did not wake. The waves continued their chant more forcefully.

"Your vessel is sinking; survive the tides.

The end is coming; open your eyes."

The boy moved again but still wouldn't wake. The crowd laughed.

After a few more attempts and bursts of laughter, a girl ran on the stage with the wooden cut-out of an Albertosaurus that I had spotted earlier outside my window. She let out a loud scream right next to the sleeper. The crowd laughed hysterically as the noise startled the boy, and he almost fell out of the boat. He balanced himself clumsily and looked around, acting scared.

Then he checked his watch and searched his pockets. He found the poem and read it out loud confusingly. He looked around, scratching his head with a puzzled expression on his face, rocking in the boat comically.

The entire village laughed, and I laughed with them.

The boy in the boat leaned forward as he spotted something in the distance. With squinted eyes, he kept looking ahead.

Gradually, the waves started walking off the stage to one side, and from the other side came the trees. The newcomer watched them in amazement. He left the boat, which started heading back and out the same way as the waves. From behind the trees appeared people of the island who greeted him warmly.

It was my story, but also everyone else's story. I knew this part but was eager to see what would happen next, so I watched the performance expectantly.

The music became more dramatic, and another newcomer dressed in identical clothes ran out from behind the boy in the boat. I hadn't noticed that they were not one but two boys—or at some point, another one had somehow snuck in and hid behind the first one.

The people who had come to greet the boy moved back and watched the boys silently.

The first boy began to water a tree while the other picked a flower and crushed it under his feet. The first one shook his head in disapproval, but the second one laughed carefree.

Dejected, the first one went back to watering another tree. The cruel one formed a fireball and threw it toward the tree. The unfortunate tree immediately turned into burnt char.

It reminded me of the burnt part of the island that I had seen from my boat. They must have been telling a true story.

The kind boy stared at the other one furiously, but the vile boy was not affected and kept laughing in an evil manner. The first one moved forward. The other stepped forward proudly. Now, they were going in circles. Their worried expressions hinted that something awful was about to happen.

They lunged at each other, and a fight started. It went on for some time. Eventually, both fell to the ground and lay motionless. The people who stood behind the trees ran toward the kind boy and were amazed as flowers from the nearby trees began to fall over his body. He moved slowly and, in a moment, was sitting up, all fine and healthy. The crowd cheered and clapped in excitement.

The evil boy was still motionless on the ground. Some villagers carried him to a boat and put him in.

The good boy was now standing in the center of the stage. He pointed at the one in the boat and sang:

"I tell you the tale of a miserable soul;

Incarnation of greed, a foolish mole.

Rejected tradition, fell from grace;

His pride, no longer, could he brace.

Reason or caution was not his aim,

But disgust and slur and disdain.

A heart so dark, no light could save.

Destroy the ark, a mission he made.

Blind with hate, he chose a foul play.

Grim his fate, he had to pay.

Pride is hexing, slander and poison;

Let this be a warning, reminder, and lesson."

The waves carried the boat away. The crowd went ecstatic as it left the stage.

All the characters came back for a final bow. I clapped and cheered and appreciated them along with the entire village.

The music stopped, and a girl arrived on the stage, walking slowly till she stood in the center, looking over the crowd. She spoke in a dramatic, thundering voice:

"Mysterious start and options countless,

Greedy and proud or caring boundless.

Steal and offend or heal and mend;

What path you intend, my new friend?

The history we witnessed, not worth a repeat.

The comer we observed; a person so sweet.

A thinking mind,

A being so kind,

Has secrets to find,

And release our bind.

This one is a thinker, fair assessment decrees,

Like blessed ones who taught us the magic of trees,

Still only a seed and time he will need

To unravel the mysteries, a wondrous deed.

The mission is noble and riddles to beat

I wish you the best; it's no simple feat."

The crowd cheered and whistled as Aymelek whispered in my ear, "Congratulations, you have been chosen to be a thinker. You should stand up and thank the people."

I stood up and looked from one side to the other, bowing

my head in respect and appreciation. The crowd responded with claps and whistles.

Music started playing again, and a girl named Sanam sang in her mesmerizing voice. People danced to the rhythmic beating of drums, chatting happily. Many of them came over and introduced themselves. The rest of the day passed in introductions and merry laughter.

I liked meeting Fabio and Misa the most. Aymelek said that both of them had been friends since they met. Fabio was thin and tall with a broad mischievous smile. His eyes sparkled as he laughed loudly at every small thing. Misa was equally fun but quite the opposite in appearance as she was much shorter than Fabio. Framed by her long red curls, her face shone brightly as she talked nonstop. Aymelek left me with them and went around talking to others. I spent most of the evening with them. They showed me their favorite trail, right in the village center, around the magical trees and back. The trees glowed in the dark, lighting the path in a rainbow of colors. It was an incredible sight. I wanted to know about the trees and their magic, but they said Aymelek would tell me in detail.

When Aymelek returned to us, she was happy to see me chatting with my new friends. After some time, Fabio and Misa left. I sat with Aymelek watching the people laughing merrily, and thought about my work as a Thinker. My mind was full of questions. I had no idea what a thinker was supposed to do. Aymelek sensed my preoccupation and asked what was bothering me. I told her. She replied gently, "Do not worry, I will answer all your questions. We still have another day to spend together. The orientation for newcomers lasts for two days."

After the party, I returned to my room in the lodge. I couldn't wait to wake up in the morning and learn more about this island, but it was pretty difficult to fall asleep. I stayed up late, as my mind was busy with excitement, still not fully believing all the wonderful things that had happened during the day. I pondered over the actions of the two boys portrayed in the performance and promised myself that I would live just like the kind one. The play on the stage hinted that something terrible had happened here. I wondered who did that and why. This place was so beautiful, and the people were so kind that it was unimaginable to think someone could try to ruin it.

Chapter 3

The following day, Aymelek arrived with the same cheery look, carrying breakfast, but there was no notebook in her hand anymore. "I have good news for you," she announced, smiling broadly. "Your home is ready! You can move in today."

"So quick?" Unexpectedly, the news of getting my own place filled me with joy.

She informed me that we would see my new home after breakfast, so we ate quickly and left.

Serenus Lodge was located right next to the village center, and so far, I had not seen anything else. We followed a path away from the center with beautiful wooden homes on both sides.

All the houses were similar in size and structure. A circular fence surrounded each home with an opening in the front for a stone pathway that connected the street to the entrance door.

Every house had a front and a back yard with enough space on the sides to walk around it. The beautiful plants and trees that decorated these yards gave each house a unique look and reflected the owner's taste.

As we walked farther away from the center, I saw a glittering pond fed by a stream. Aymelek explained that the stream was coming from a nearby lake and that numerous bodies of water littered the island, but they didn't join the water surrounding it.

Once I understood the basic layout of the village, I asked Aymelek about the magical trees. She replied, "I can show you the trees another day. You will have to experience the magic yourself. Words can not explain how amazing they are."

"Alright. What is a thinker? What am I supposed to do?"

"A thinker is a person who explores the concepts and workings of things and how we can use the understanding to our advantage. The thinkers of the past figured out how to use the power of the magical trees. There are still so many unanswered questions. Thinkers focus on those questions and try to find an answer through experimentation and research."

"So, what questions am I supposed to find the answers to?"

She laughed at my question. "It is entirely up to you. You will encounter many mysteries. You can choose the ones that interest you. But it's too early yet, and you have a lot of time to figure things out. Explore the village and the forest. See what captures your curious mind."

"I wish I knew which question I was supposed to answer. It would have been easier that way."

"It will take time. Let it come to you. Until then, just enjoy this place, make friends and learn what we already know."

"What about the mystery of where we come from?" I knew this was a tricky question, and as soon as I asked about it, I doubted if I could ever find an answer.

Aymelek felt the same and said, "That is a big ask. There are no clues. Where would you even start? I would advise you to leave this particular question. There are so many things that can make people's lives better. Work on those." She paused and looked at me, trying to judge how I was taking it, then continued, "Start with smaller things, and then maybe one day you will be able to find the answers to the big questions too."

By then, we had reached a wooden boardwalk, and across it stood a single house on a slightly raised mound with no other buildings in sight. In the front was a low-lying swamp with overgrown grass that took over most of the land, extending to the bottom of a steep hill farther away. Behind the house was a slightly raised but muddy forest.

Aymelek told me that this was my home. I was shocked to see the place. I had seen so many houses in such beautiful places on my way here that the view of my house lowered my spirits badly. It could have easily been the worst place for a home. The look on Aymelek's face told me that she felt the same. We had just crossed a river a few moments ago. It had flowed so gracefully, and I wished I could get a house where I could hear the water running over the rocks.

It was hard to be happy about this place, but I forced an awkward smile and went inside to inspect my home. I tried to show as much enthusiasm as possible, but I was sure Aymelek could see through it.

Inside the home, a large window gave a plentiful view of the swamp and the hillside. Further ahead in the corner was a stone fireplace facing the open space in the center with two chairs on a circular rug. There were no rooms there like the ones in the lodge. A table and a chair were arranged right underneath a raised wooden bed. It was simple but comfortable.

Aymelek was equally troubled by the surroundings of the house, but she reminded me that the process of allocating a piece of land to a newcomer was fair. I had received the next available spot.

She tried to point out a few benefits of the place to make me feel better. She said that thinkers usually preferred a peaceful environment, and since it was extremely muddy around the home, there was no chance of more houses being built around it, so I had the whole place to myself.

She was trying to cheer me up, but there was no denying it. I had received a swampy yard with no other homes around for company. I tried to tell her that it was alright, although I didn't believe my own words.

Changing the topic, she showed me a frame hanging on the wall. It had the poem that the girl on the stage had read to declare that I would be a thinker. It was carved on wood and was a gift from Kratos. I remembered the kind blacksmith I had met on my arrival. He showed his kindness once again through his gift.

Aymelek looked out of the window facing the backyard and pointed outside. "Your boat is in your backyard." I walked to the window and looked out, repeating her words in my mind: *Your backyard.* It was my backyard. I felt an association with the place and was happy that I had a home. Soon, I had forgotten all about the swamp.

Aymelek showed me how to start a fire in the fireplace. Then she pointed at a cabinet and said, "Pots and pans are in there. If you need something else, you can ask Kratos. He will help you."

I could see firewood on the bottom shelf of the cabinet. Then I pulled on a hinged door above it. Inside, I found pots and pans and some more utensils.

Aymelek pointed to the table under the bed. "You will find paper and pen over there. Aidas makes paper from all kinds of plant fibers. You can go to her if you need more."

I nodded, grateful for the care they had shown me. Everything they thought I could need had been taken care of. I was being cared for and was welcome here. It felt great.

Aymelek offered to teach me how to make tea. She took some dry leaves from a jar and said, "These are creeping snowberry leaves. Boiling these in the water releases a minty flavor, which makes an excellent tasting tea, and adding a few drops of lemon can further enhance the taste." Then she added knowingly, "It is good for headaches too. It is a common plant in the area. You can pick the leaves in the forest."

When the tea was ready, I tasted it. It was minty and refreshing. I studied the leaves carefully so I could spot them in the forest by myself.

The orientation was coming to an end, and I had started to

get anxious that soon I would be left on my own to figure things out. Aymelek informed me about many people who could help me with various problems.

She concluded the topic with: "You can eat at the village center, but most people like to prepare their own breakfast in the comfort of their homes. The cooks at the village kitchen can tell you the recipes to make a simple and healthy breakfast."

A loud knock rapped at my door. I opened it and was delighted to find Fabio and Misa. They had arrived carrying some blankets and pillows. It was a gift from Azar, the wool maker.

Fabio and Misa worked at the forge. They didn't stay long, as they had taken a short break from work. They invited me to visit them at their workplace and left looking around dismissively. Obviously, they did not like the look of the area surrounding my home either.

Aymelek put out the fire and stood up. She wanted me to go with her for the last part of the orientation. We were going to both ends of the island.

First, she took me to where I had come from. We stood at the edge of the water. Then, she picked up a stick and hurled it in the air. It flew forward for a bit, then hit an invisible barrier and came flying back. She pulled me down just in time as the stick zoomed over my head. It was fun. We laughed as we threw many things at the invisible wall, and every time, they bounced back, and we had to jump and duck to avoid getting hit.

Aymelek told me that it was one of the games that people played here. It was just harmless fun. She held my hand, and we walked in the water to the invisible barrier. We could go no farther. A spongy force pushed us back. The more we pushed forward, the more it resisted.

"It's time to go to the other side," Aymelek announced. "But before that, let's eat at the village center. The walk to the other side is longer, and the trip would take us the rest of the day."

After the meal, we walked a twisty path running parallel to the river beyond the fall. I spotted a few bridges over the river, but we stayed on track. We met many Seren on our way there. They were coming back from the Dark End—that was what they called the island's edge on that side.

Once we reached our destination, I figured out why they called it that. The barrier here was like a thick, foggy black wall. We could see nothing past it.

I found people playing here as well, but the game was different. Instead of bouncing back, the thrown things made a swishing noise as they went through the barrier and were carried forward and away from the island.

Aymelek threw a stone. It made a whistling noise and gradually slowed down to match the speed of the invisible current, and then it carried on at a constant speed till it disappeared.

The current carried the rocks thrown in the water while the invisible wind took the things thrown in the air. And soon after they breached the barrier, they became invisible in the black fog. All we could see ahead of us was complete and utter darkness.

A person brought some garbage and threw it in the water.

Aymelek told me this was how they kept the island clean. The water carried all undesirable things away.

We threw some sticks and stones and found it quite entertaining. The swishing sound was pleasing to the ear. I found myself wanting to do it over and over again.

Aymelek reminded me, "Remember not to go in the current. We can walk forward but cannot come back."

With that, the orientation was over, and after having some more fun at the Dark End, we returned to the village center. The sun was setting by the time we arrived. We ate one last meal together.

Starting tomorrow, I was supposed to be on my own, without a guide. Aymelek left after dinner but invited me to come to her whenever I needed help. I was grateful for her kindness and thanked her enthusiastically.

After she left, I sat alone and looked around nervously for some time. There was a whole world around me. I could go anywhere and do anything, but I felt empty and lonely. What was I supposed to do? I decided I would head home before it was too dark. The long walk back to my lone house further reminded me of my loneliness.

I did not feel ready to be on my own yet. The walk in the dark scared me, and I found myself going faster and faster. By the time I reached home, I was so scared that I kept feeling that someone—or something—was following me. I knew there was no one there. Still, I couldn't push the thought out of my head. Fear quickened my steps. Every small sound made me jump and look over my shoulder fearfully. My heart beat loudly against my chest. I hugged myself defensively as the distinctive smell of the swamp reminded me of its creepy presence. I almost ran up to my door, jerked it open, rushed inside, and quickly closed the door behind me. It felt much better once I was inside the safety of the walls.

It took some time to calm myself. I started a fire with some effort, as Aymelek had shown me, and then sat on the chair facing the fireplace. Strangely, fire made me feel even safer.

When I grew tired of sitting, I went to look out of the window. The darkness was unnerving. I closed the window and moved away from it.

I was tired and sleepy, but the dark scared me. I lit a candle before putting out the fire in the fireplace and kept it burning for some time as I lay in the bed with my eyes open.

The candlelight made the home feel very cozy but scary at the same time as it cast shadows on the walls, which moved as the flame flickered. I had stayed alone at the Serenus Lodge without any fear. It was strange that I was so scared in my home.

To divert my attention, I listened to the sounds outside. These were the same sounds I had heard the previous night, but they felt more surreal this time. There was a feeling of vulnerability—unlike last night, I was not in the village center surrounded by other homes.

Earlier in the day, Aymelek had told me about the sounds of the night. I knew they came from crickets, chorus frogs, and the owls who hooted occasionally. But tonight, I could hear other sounds as well; one that sounded like a squirrel or some other rodent scurrying away in dry leaves and another one that felt like tapping or clicking, like something was bumping into another. I tried to make sense of it. There was no pattern to its repetition. In the end, I concluded that it was just the wind that caused this sound. Nothing to worry about, I thought, trying to convince myself.

When all the reasoning and convincing failed to remove my fears, I hid in the thick blankets and fell asleep.

In the morning, Kratos and Aymelek arrived with breakfast. Aymelek was worried for me. She said newcomers could feel scared to be alone in their new homes, even when surrounded by other houses. My home was isolated and near a swamp.

She was right; I had been afraid, but I didn't tell her that. I thanked Kratos for his gift of the carved poem as a hanging frame. He smiled at me but looked around angrily. He didn't approve of the location of my home either.

After breakfast, at Kratos's invitation, we walked to the village center. Aymelek left for Feray's yard while Kratos and I continued to a bigger building. Two armed men were guarding its entrance. They recognized Kratos, greeted him with respect, and moved out of the way to let us in.

Inside, we met an old lady. She had a kind and graceful face, and when she talked, her wisdom was reflected in her tone. She greeted us welcomingly, and Kratos told her about the swamp around my place. He was mad at the builders for building my home on such an undesirable site.

The old lady asked us to wait as she sent a guardian to call the builder to explain why he had chosen that location.

As we sat there waiting, Kratos invited me to his forge. He said I was welcome to go to him anytime I needed something. He told me about the kind lady, as well. She was Alev, one of the village elders. People came to her when they needed to resolve any problem.

Soon, the builder arrived. He lowered his head to greet Alev with respect. When told why we were there, he said, "Each house is to be built on the next accessible site that is big enough to accommodate the building and the yards. The pathway needs to remain clear in all seasons." He turned toward me and asked, "Is your house and the yard not the same size as others, or is it not accessible?"

Kratos interrupted him, "Why did you have to build near a swamp and where it is so far from other houses?"

The builder responded casually, "I remember the entire set of guidelines that I must follow. Nowhere am I told not to build near a swamp. There is also no mention of it needing to be close to other houses."

Kratos was not satisfied with his response. He directed his argument toward Alev. "How is this a good experience for a newcomer to live alone near a swamp? Our guidelines are supposed to be secondary. The primary goal is to provide a good experience."

The kind old lady thought for a while. Then, she asked the builder, "It's clearly not a place where you would have liked to live when you were a newcomer, right?"

The builder's face flushed with embarrassment. He nodded quietly. Since they were convinced the place was not suitable for living, I hoped they would give me a different house, but Alev's words took my hope away.

"We cannot move Seren around once a piece of land has been allotted. That will cause many to want a different house. It will bring more bad feelings than good." She turned toward me and said in a polite tone, "You will have to stay at the house that was assigned to you. I am sorry for the discomfort you have to go through, but we don't have any other option."

Then she addressed the builder and said, "You need to make sure that each next house is built in a place that does not provide such a negative experience."

In the end, she addressed Kratos, "You are a wise man, Kratos. You understand that we cannot change the allocation without creating a bigger problem. But now that this issue has been raised, it will not happen to another."

Kratos was not happy, but he understood what Alev meant. I felt dejected by the decision. But there was nothing to say. We thanked the lady and left toward the village center. Before Kratos left, he offered that he could send someone to stay with me if I was scared. He told me it could continue for a few nights till I got comfortable being alone in my home. I assured him that I was okay. I understood that this was my permanent home, and I had to get accustomed to living there by myself. I hid my fears and thanked him for his efforts.

After Kratos left, I stood alone in the village center wondering what to do. I wanted to check out my place more while there was still some light. I decided to eat my lunch and head home.

I also took some food for the night as I didn't intend to be out in the evening. The experience of the walk back to my home in the dark was not something I wanted to repeat.

There was still plenty of daylight left when I arrived home. After leaving my dinner inside, I inspected the front yard. It was devoid of any vegetation. I planned to plant some flowers there. Not today, of course. But soon enough.

I stood in the middle of the front yard and spread my wings. They pushed the air down as I flapped them, creating a loud noise. I felt lighter, but my feet did not lift off the ground. I tried a few more times but soon got tired.

I was puzzled as to why we had wings if we couldn't fly. Another mystery to be solved.

I walked to my front door and sat down. The cattail grass in the swamp swayed lightly in the wind. The place had an eerie feeling to it. After sitting there aimlessly for a little while, I went inside and made tea.

Then, while enjoying tea, I inspected the backyard. A stone pathway led from the front door to the side and back, reaching the center of the backyard. All around, wild vegetation grew. My boat was tied to a fence post using a metal chain. The wooden fence was erected recently, which disturbed the vegetation. But other than that, the yard was covered in overgrown foliage. I made a mental note to clean up this place. Not today, but sometime soon.

After leaving the empty cup inside, I walked across the wooden boardwalk toward the newer houses. These were still vacant and to be awarded to the next newcomers.

I felt jealous. These houses looked very safe and inviting compared to mine. I wished I had come after just one more newcomer. Then I would have lived here instead.

I kept walking on the path till it ended near a forest. Builders had not yet cleared this area. I spotted some snowberry plants and picked a handful of leaves. Then I returned home, washed the leaves, and left them out to dry.

With nothing else to do, I sat on a chair and listened to the wind outside. It was a windy day and was turning into a stormy one, which made it impossible to do anything outside. I decided that I would go out and meet other Seren tomorrow and see what exciting things could interest me. I needed to find a stimulating question to answer.

Outside, the wind got louder and louder. And then came the rain. It was amazing. The raindrops fell on the roof in a continuous volley of musical notes. I stood in the window and enjoyed my first rain as it got heavier and heavier.

When the rain started, everything else had gone quiet. The critters that lived in the swamp were silent. I thought they must be enjoying the sound of the howling wind and the rain splattering in the mud.

Earlier, when I was bored, I had hoped that someone would come to visit me, but now, I didn't expect to see anyone due to the weather.

Gradually, it turned dark and cold, so I started a fire and noticed that soon, I would need to get more wood. I had to figure out where I could find it.

I picked a paper and pen and prepared a list of things I needed to do, chores necessary to maintain my home, and all the unanswered questions I had come across so far.

Then, on a new piece of paper, I wrote:

All of us come in a boat carrying only a poem and a watch. We have wings, but we can not fly. We do not know where we come from or what is next. And we do not know why we are here. We can live here, grow old, and then die.

I know things that no one told me. I know the names of things, I know that it is raining outside, and I know how to write and that I can write on paper with a pen, but I don't know many other things, like why I have a watch that shows a whirlpool. And how did I know that it was called a whirlpool?

I need to find out how I know the things I know. And I need to find out the things I do not know.

I took the paper with the poem out of my pocket and read it a few times. Then I placed it on the table with other notes.

After that, I settled in the chair, looking at the fireplace listening to the sounds of the rain outside, and realized that Aymelek's assessment was correct. I was a thinker. I needed to know things that I didn't know. Not knowing bothered me. But maybe it bothered others as well; it was possible that everybody thought about these things but never found the answers.

I had to find the answers. It was my job.

I recalled the poem and decided to ask others what they thought it meant. It clearly sounded like a mission, instructions I needed to follow. But Aymelek had said that it was not the case.

The weather continued into the morning, and I woke up to the noise of the wind and rain. I had nothing to eat for breakfast. Aymelek had been bringing it every day, but now I had to do it myself.

I made tea with the last of the firewood and waited for the rain to stop. Looking outside the window, the low-lying swamp was filling up with water. More and more water flowed down the hillside. Soon, I could only see the tips of the cattail grass.

I checked the boardwalk. It was still above the surface of the water. If the rain didn't stop, it could submerge the path. The thought scared me, but I reminded myself that at least I had a boat.

There was no telling how long it would take for the rain to stop. I needed to be better prepared, so I made a list of things to always have in the home so that even if the rain cut me off from the rest of the village, I could survive without facing any problems.

Food was on top of the list. Firewood, as well.

Thankfully, the rain stopped soon, and I headed out for the midday meal.

I met the cook in the kitchen, who was kind enough to show me how to prepare my breakfast. It was quite simple. Every meal consisted of bread, vegetables, and fruit. Herbs and spices added flavor to the food. The recipes were easy to make. He gave me enough dry ingredients to last a few days.

Firewood was collected and dried at a nearby stockpile. I carried some in a cart and then dropped the cart back.

Next, I went to the magical trees to meet Aymelek, but she wasn't there.

Feray met me at the door of her house as she was heading out. I was hesitant to ask about her work because of her cold behavior a few days ago, but I was too curious to let the opportunity go. I picked up courage and asked, "Can you tell me about the magical trees, Feray?"

She responded half-heartedly, "Yes, I can, but let's be quick about it. I have a lot to do." I followed her like an unwanted guest.

We stopped before entering the circle of trees. Feray said, "These are Lighttrees. The seven trees circle around the white one - the Moontree. Each of these produces different colored flowers and has a unique magical effect. Six of the trees in the outer circle are the same size, but the seventh has only two trunks and forms an arch that serves as the entrance to the circle. As you can see, the Moontree is much larger and taller. It is the one that other trees rely on. We believe it is the mother, and the seven are its children."

We walked to the arched entrance. The branches overhead

tangled into each other. Unlike other trees, the flowers on the arch tree were in a gradient of colors. The color changed from indigo to violet to red.

The entrance opened into a spacious yard that I had walked on with Fabio and Misa. This area formed the inner circle around the Moontree. Each of the six trees had an opening facing the inner circle, and to our right was the tree with red flowers.

Feray walked toward it and went inside. I followed. The first thing I noticed was that it was not a single tree. Six trunks stood like sturdy pillars, expanding the ceiling formed by the inter-twined branches to its incredible width. These pillars made a circle around an open, brighter area.

In the center was a bulb—a single massive fruit. It sat on the ground, and branches from all six trees around it came to it from above and hung it, just barely touching the ground. Sur-rounding it were tables and benches. I went closer for a better look. It glowed and emitted a red light, bathing everything in a soft, fiery hue.

I looked around in disbelief as Feray explained, "The flowers on the six pillar trees collect the light and store it in the bulb in the middle. People sit on the benches and absorb the light to receive each tree's magical benefit. Except for the entrance arch, each tree is the same. A bulb in the middle, surrounded by a seating area which is encircled by the six tree trunks." She pointed to the shelves between the trees. "One opening to walk into the tree chamber, and the rest are filled with shelves to store the light vials we collect."

I looked around. Tall, wooden, backless shelves joined each tree trunk, leaving one opening from where we came into the tree chamber. Hundreds of glass vials glowing with the red contents lined the shelves neatly.

The vials attracted my curiosity, and without thinking, I went closer and touched one.

"Careful! It's fragile and very precious," Feray said urgently.

I pulled my hand back and stood away from the shelf. "What are these?"

"These vials have the sunset light in them. To keep safe until we need to use it. The trees continuously collect the light in the bulb until it is full. But when there is no sun for a few days, the bulb loses its glow and needs to be refilled. It is my job to collect more light in the vials for when the tree runs out or if I need to use it away from the tree."

"Sunset light? In a vial?"

Feray answered while carefully arranging the already organized vials. "The light of the sun when it sets. Where else would you put light except in a glass vial?"

I couldn't believe what she said. It seemed to battle everything I knew, but then again, how much *did* I know? "We can store light in glass vials?"

"Not everyone can do it, but I can. Though it is not easy—the timing is critical. A little early or a little late, and you will get the wrong color. I have to wait patiently until it is the right shade. The sun gives this particular hue for a cruelly short time."

Feray's demeanor went through a surprising change. First, she was cold, but now she was very excited and happy as she started telling me about her work. She seemed pretty proud of it. I liked this side of her.

She took a tiny vial from a shelf and held it in front of me. "This is how much I get in one sunset." The vial was smaller than my palm. I glanced at the shelves and wondered how long it must have taken her to collect this much light.

"What do you do with it?" I asked.

"I am a healer. I use the lights to heal the Seren."

"Healing by sunlight? How is it possible?" it was all very complicated. She could capture sunlight, store it, and use it to heal others.

She put the vial back and said, "The sun gives life to the living. It can also heal. I collect and use the lights to heal people." She spread her arms to point at the trees and said, "Don't they grow from a tiny seed into these giants in the presence of sunlight? Can any living thing go on its journey of life without it? No sunlight means no life. The Redlight helps heal the ailments of the blood. If someone loses blood, the sunset light will help them regain it quickly."

Feray had now transformed into an enthusiastic teacher. "Come. I will show you the other lights I have collected. You will be amazed to know what they can do." She put the little vial back, and we went out. Next, it was the Orangetree.

We entered the chamber. It was a complete replica of the red one, except for the color of the flowers, the hues emanating from the fruit bulb, and the matching glowing vials. It was equally mesmerizing. I watched the bulb in the center with swirls of orange light inside as Feray said, "Orangelight gives strength to mind and body."

Feray continued as we approached the Yellowtree. "These trees are ancient. Who planted them and when is a part of lost history. They have been helping the healers for as long as we remember. Yellowlight strengthens creativity and imagination. Thinkers prefer to spend time in its chambers when they need to think outside the box."

These mysterious ancient trees fascinated me. I was especially happy to know about the Yellowtree and decided to visit it soon. It might push my imagination enough to come up with a question worth thinking about.

The next tree that we visited was green. I was surprised to see green flowers. Somehow, I had strongly associated green with leaves, and seeing green flowers was a remarkable experience.

Feray told me about the healing effects of the Greenlight. "Green brings clarity to the mind. It is another tree that thinkers like to spend time in. Sitting under the Yellowtree can make your thoughts a bit too adventurous, taking you to strange places. I recommend visiting the Greentree afterward to find clarity in your new imagination. Thinkers can receive this tree's benefit much more than others, and it allows them to understand concepts that may otherwise seem beyond their ability."

I listened to the information attentively and realized that visiting these majestic trees was a part of my work. I looked forward to coming here often. I knew I would love it. Not just for my work but also to cherish the beauty of this place. With another look at the vials of the cool Greenlight, I walked out after Feray.

Then we visited the blue chamber, and Feray asked me how I felt. I knew why she asked that. We had just come in, but I had felt different almost immediately. Calm and peaceful. The feeling struck me. I told her so, and she was satisfied to hear the answer.

"Yes, Bluelight brings peace of mind. The lights do not just heal the body, they also heal the soul, and different lights affect us in different ways. The villagers come here often to sit under the trees. They stay in the chambers, and these lights heal them, uplift their moods, tame their tempers, enhance imagination, provide clarity of thought, and make them energetic."

The mysterious ancient trees fascinated and surprised me. They probably intrigued Feray even more. I asked her why she became a healer.

"Being a healer is not a choice. I had the ability, and so this is my job. Aymelek also has the ability, but she is still learning," Feray explained as we entered the last tree in the circle—the Indigotree.

It reminded me of the tree on the island under the waterfall, which was used as my prison room, though it couldn't keep me in. It had seemed absurd to use such a place as a prison. I wanted to ask Feray about it but didn't want to interrupt her, so I left the question for later.

"What does this light do?" I asked instead.

"Indigolight gives self-control. This tree can be very helpful for people who have trouble organizing themselves." Her rushed answer made me feel she didn't seem very impressed by the healing effect of this tree.

"What time do you collect this light?" I asked.

"At midday. The sun shines brightly right above the water-falls. It is reflected off the clear blue water and falls on the water tree to produce this light."

Aymelek's voice suddenly interrupted us. "Feray! Where are you?"

We walked out of the tree chamber. I greeted Aymelek—she smiled back and then spoke to Feray, "Kratos says the project is on schedule. He wanted to know if you would like to come and make sure things were going in the right direction. And he wanted me to send the newcomer over to his forge."

We had seen all the tree chambers except the white one. It stood tall in the middle, surrounded by other large trees, still overshadowing them with its expansive size.

Feray looked at the Moontree. I followed her eyes, hoping she would show me its chamber. The white flowers shone in the bright sunlight, giving it an ethereal glow. To my disappoint-ment, she turned away from it and walked to her home outside the Tree Circle. Aymelek and I followed her to the wooden house.

A small garden separated the front yard from the outer yard

that contained all the colorful trees. A wooden fence surrounded it, enclosing a grassy patch with wildflowers.

The path led to the front door of the house. A flowering vine occupied the wall on the right of the entrance, spreading to the roof. A window on the left wall overlooked the front garden. This house was much larger than the others, and the wooden door and window had intricate designs carved on them. It was old, but the excellent condition and the well-kept garden reflected the love and care given by the inhabitants.

I wondered what lay inside its ancient walls and waited for Feray to invite me in, but she didn't.

As we reached the door, she turned around and stood in front of the door facing us. After an awkward moment, she said, "I have work to do. Go with Aymelek. She will take you to Kratos."

I thanked her for showing me the Tree Circle, turned around, and left with Aymelek.

Aymelek and I walked toward the village center. She pointed to a path and said, "Kratos's forge is through there. I need to get back to Feray. Do you think you can go by yourself? Just follow the path, and you will be there. It isn't too long."

I told her not to worry and thanked her. I walked the path for a few moments. The sounds of hammering and clanking of metal tools indicated that the forge was nearby.

Soon, I reached an open area with a large workshop and a hearth in the center. Two long buildings with large verandas were visible at the back. Kratos was busy working with another man. They were taking turns hammering a long piece of metal. He saw me coming and left his work to greet me.

"How's it going?" he asked. I liked the way he talked to me—gently. Most people were generous and welcoming, but Kratos was more so than the others.

We made our path between the metal structures occupying the forge as he led me on a tour of the place. Many people were working at different stations, busy building new metal parts. He introduced me to his apprentice, Idir, a strong-looking young man with a big smile, and then we went out in the yard.

One building at the back was the armory, but I was surprised to find no weapons there. Kratos explained, "We used to make weapons and armor in the past, but they are not needed anymore. The guardians already have everything they need. Occasionally, someone comes with a loose joint or a broken chain, and we fix it, but that's all. We are using the armory to store our tools and raw materials."

The other building was used to store firewood and coal.

With this, the tour ended, and we went back to Idir. He was still hammering the iron piece, flattening it into a rectangle. I watched him work for a while and then looked at the strange gold and silver structures piling up all around the work area.

Kratos explained, "We are working on a big project that Feray designed. And it's about the right time too. We were getting bored of doing the routine things over and over again."

"But what is it?"

He laughed. "I have been wondering the same thing. Feray didn't explain it. She just sent me the designs. She says it is supposed to be a surprise."

"She calls it her special project," Idir added, joining the conversation. "We are very excited to see how it turns out."

Kratos and Idir went back to work.

As I walked around the place, I met Fabio. He was working on a part and stopped when he saw me. I didn't want to bother him, but he did not seem to mind and walked with me to a side where they had some chairs and a table. We sat down. Misa ran over to join us. They were always together. She greeted me and asked how things were going.

We chatted for a little while, then I asked them about their thoughts about where we came from and what was beyond the island.

Fabio replied, "No one knows for sure, but everyone has a theory. If you want to hear the most interesting ones, you should go to Qilam. He was a thinker..."

Misa interrupted him, "Qilam has gone crazy. You want him to talk to *him* for answers?"

Fabio clarified defensively, "No, I am just saying that he is really passionate about these questions and has amazing theories." Then he looked at me and said, "But don't believe his words. These questions have made him a little soft in the head."

Misa added, "I don't think you should be talking to Qilam at all. There are so many questions to answer. Find out things that will actually help people."

Obviously, now I wanted to meet Qilam, however crazy he may sound. I needed to know what he knew to separate the crazy from facts myself.

Dark clouds covered the sun. I could hear a distant rumble. "I think it will rain again today," I said.

"The rainy season is starting. You should get used to it," Fabio said.

Misa added, "Do you have an umbrella?" I shook my head. She continued, "You should get one. I think I have one here that you can take."

She went to get an umbrella, and Fabio gave me my first task. "You are a thinker. Can you think of something for me?" I nodded gladly. He continued, "I work at the forge. I like it, but sometimes I wonder if it's the right job for me. Can you tell me how to know if this is what I'm supposed to do?"

I was surprised at his question but was happy to have something to think about. I never thought I would be thinking about such questions. I was more interested in the bigger mysteries that surrounded the island. Still, I promised him that I would think about it and return to him with an answer.

Misa was back. I thanked them and left for home, taking the umbrella with me. The day was almost over, and it was getting dark.

At home, I prepared tea to warm myself up after dinner. I left the fireplace burning for as long as I was awake. Then, I listened to the sounds of crickets as I lay in bed, thinking about the magical trees and the colorful lights. And, most important-ly, about meeting Qilam. I reminded myself not to believe in whatever he was going to tell me, to just take it as the opinion of a person who could be totally wrong.

Chapter 4

In the morning, I headed out to the village center and asked around to find out where I could find Qilam. Everyone I talked to was surprised I wanted to meet him. Most said it wasn't worth it. It felt like they were trying to protect me from something he might say, but this made me want to meet him even more. What were people so afraid of? Words didn't scare me. I knew it was my choice to believe him or not.

I learned that Qilam no longer lived in his home. He abandoned it a few weeks ago and lived in the deeper part of the forest, as he preferred to be alone. He used to be a thinker like me, but his thoughts had become unbearable for people. Gradually, he moved away.

Finally, the cook in the village kitchen provided the information I was looking for. He told me that I could find him on a walking trail that led to the deep forest. He asked if I could take some food for Qilam, as he had not come in for some in the past few days. I was happy to help. I took the food and left for the trail in the forest.

The Seren probably came here often. The trail was easy to follow even as it twisted and curved around the trees. The dense tree canopies above me didn't let much sunlight reach the ground, and the vegetation was sparse. The forest was more open than I expected. Looking from outside, it looked much more thickly populated, but once I had walked for a bit, there were a lot of open spaces, although the sky was barely visible.

A constant hum surrounded me as I continued walking the trail, looking for Qilam. It was the sound of the wind, birds, and bugs - the sounds of life in a living forest. I had never asked anyone if there were dangerous animals in the woods, and the thought bothered me now that I was all alone.

Thankfully, it wasn't long before I found Qilam sitting under a huge tree. He was old but looked even older than his age. An unkempt beard and messy hair made him look like a sad, dejected fellow. When he saw me, his eyes lit up. He must have been happy to meet someone after staying away from people for days.

I told him I brought food and sat by as he ate. I could tell that he was hungry. Still, he was more interested in talking. I told him that I was a newcomer and was supposed to be a thinker. He looked up at me, staring right in my eyes, paused for a bit, and said, "There are many better things to do. Don't be a thinker."

I didn't expect this answer. "Why not? I like to know things."

He replied, "Everyone likes to know things. What are you interested in knowing?"

I was hoping the conversation would lead to this. I seized the opportunity and said, "I want to know why we came to this island and what is next. And where do we come—"

"People already blame me for Alfred. Do you want me to get in more trouble?"

"Alfred? Who is Alfred?" I asked.

"Who was Alfred? He was a brilliant young man, but he is gone now. Didn't they tell you about him?" I shook my head, and he continued, "He was a woodworker. The best there ever was. Someone so young rarely gets this good at something. And even though he wasn't a thinker, he liked to know things."

"Then what happened?" I sensed sadness in his words.

"He made the biggest boat he could make and left the island in search of what is next. You see, people think I filled his head with these ideas. No, he was way ahead of me in his passion for finding out if there were more islands ahead of us."

He seemed to be regretting something, or maybe he was defending himself against what others thought of him.

Qilam continued, "The entire village thinks he left because of his conversations with me. They don't believe me that it wasn't the case. Didn't they try to stop you from meeting me?"

I told him the truth about how people thought his ideas were crazy and that I shouldn't believe what he had to say.

He laughed. "Yeah, crazy theories to explain a crazy world. Maybe the people are right. You are too young; you shouldn't be worrying about these things."

"Listening to someone's opinion about things is not danger-ous. No one can force me into believing something I don't want to believe in, and I only believe in things that make sense to me."

He laughed heartily and said, "Ideas can be scary. You are too young to understand. An idea can cut deeper than the sharpest sword. Words are powerful." He paused and then continued in a firm tone, "With words, you can motivate people to believe in lies. You already believe in many lies that they have been telling you. It's amazing how we are so blind and yet so proud of our beliefs."

I was confused. Was I proud and blind? "What do you mean? What lies?"

"Go and live an easy life. Don't get entangled in these questions." He tried to push me away, but now I wanted to know even more.

"The more you hide, the more I want to know. If you do not tell me, I will talk to someone else."

He replied knowingly, "I know the type. The need to know." He sighed loudly and then continued, "But if you talk to them, they will only tell you lies."

"Who are they?" I asked.

"All of Serenus. The villagers. Every one of them has either been brainwashed or is on the mission to tell lies."

My curiosity was piqued. I needed to know what lies he was talking about.

I begged, "Tell me the truth then."

He frowned and watched me with sharp eyes for some time.

I could see that he was fighting an inner struggle about whether to tell me or not. He stayed quiet for a moment, but then sat up and said, "Do you know the story of the evil wizard?"

"No."

He breathed out a deep sigh. "A powerful wizard lives on this island. His magical abilities are so great that he evades death. Nothing can kill him. He has been caught many times and has been killed too. But he comes back. His goal is to send people in search of more islands. People say he steals the souls of the unfortunate ones who fall for his tricks, and that is why he cannot be killed. The poem mentions him, remember? 'Catch the wizard, go past the fall.' So many have tried to catch him, thinking it would lead them to another land past the fall. Of course, no one who went can come back to tell us if they did find a new world."

He stopped and found me waiting intently to hear more. "I believe, and mind you, I am not the only one—many have believed that there is more to this world than we understand. Gods have created more lands, and our purpose is to find a way to those islands. Only the chosen few will ever reach the end. Why else would the gods give us the poem?"

"I don't know. It must mean something." This was all I could say for sure.

"Exactly. The villagers want you to live here as if that is the purpose of life. That doesn't make any sense. Why would the gods send us a poem that says your world is so vast?" His voice was full of passion now.

His words were so confident that they puzzled me. Why didn't anyone tell me about the evil wizard? But then, Qilam might really be crazy. Or he might be tricking me with his words. I didn't know if I could believe him, but I wanted to know what more he had to say.

"What do you think the gods are telling us?" I asked.

He continued in the same passionate tone, "Think about it. Someone created us. They sent us in a boat, and the only things they gave us were a poem and a watch. Why? If I send someone to a world, why would I give them these things to start with? Right? Because they hide answers in them. I would want them to find their way forward by following the instructions in the poem. Now, this is where most people differ from my views. I don't think the poem contains hidden clues or a riddle that needs to be solved. No, the gods wanted to make it easy to understand, so they wrote it simply. I think that the poem's meaning is understood by reading it literally. Our vessel is sinking. This one is obvious. It's not the boat, or they would have said our boat is sinking. The vessel is another word for our body. It's the body that is dying. Surviving the tides means lasting long enough to reach what is next. Some people say tides are the hardships we face in our life; I think it's the tides, literally. I think the waves are bigger ahead of this island, so we need to prepare to survive those dangerous waters." He stopped and checked to see if I was following. I nodded, and he continued, "The end is coming; open your eyes—this part is a warning that we will not live forever. Our vessel is sinking, after all. Then it tells us to 'live and think, but don't you stall.' We are supposed to do something and not take too long to do it. And what is it that we need to do? 'Catch the wizard, go past the fall.' Is it just a coincidence that a wizard lives here? No! We are supposed to catch him and go forward."

I interrupted his enthusiastic speech. "Why do you think people don't believe in all this?"

His excited tone was replaced with a somber one. "They have given up. So many used to believe it, but when the wizard proved too powerful to be captured or killed, they started to think that the poem was misleading and the mission was impossible. I don't blame them. We have caught the wizard so many times. We kept him in the prison tree under the fall, but we didn't know what to do with him. He would come back if we killed him or sent him in the dark. Eventually, people stopped believing, and now no one is trying to catch the wizard. And when we are not trying to capture him, he is not attacking us either, so there is peace. Villagers prefer peace over finding answers."

"But you think we should believe in the poem?" I asked.

"Yes, but I am not claiming to understand it fully. Alfred thought we were supposed to go past the fall since we had already captured the wizard many times. He was a woodworker. He built the biggest boat he could and left the island searching for another land." Qilam's voice became sad.

"You think he made a mistake?" I asked.

He responded grimly, "I don't know. It's possible I am wrong about it and that I encouraged Alfred to go into the Dark End. It weighs heavily on my conscience that he may have died in vain. He was friends with Feray's apprentice. Everyone listens to what they think, so they say my words are dangerous for peace on the island. I try to stay away unless someone wants to know what I think because, you know, there is a good chance that what I am saying is right. This island could be a stepping stone to more amazing worlds ahead."

"Where is the wizard now?"

"I believe he is still here, hiding and scheming. He keeps trying to find a way to go forward. While he is mighty in his abilities, you should know that he is basically a coward. He wants others to try to go forward in unique new ways, and only when he is sure that it works will he go forward himself." Qilam finished the story and asked me to head back to the village before it got too dark.

I wanted to hear more, but I did not want to roam in the forest after dark. I left with my head full of new answers and even more questions.

I reached home and stayed in for the rest of the evening, thinking about Qilam's words. If he was right, this world was a temporary place, and we were supposed to go to the next one. But that was risky. It would be a safer choice to stay here, but then I may never find the answers.

After thinking for hours, I decided I was too young to go on a mission to find new lands. It was a fact, after all, that even the critters in the swamp scared me at night. Catching a powerful wizard and discovering new worlds seemed an impossible task for me.

I stopped thinking about these matters, but before that, I wrote down my newfound understanding on a piece of paper.

Qilam thinks gods have sent us with a mission. We need to catch the wizard and go past the fall looking for new worlds. We are not supposed to stay here for long. The waves ahead are bigger and more dangerous, so Alfred made a big boat and left in it. He may have died, or he may have found the answers he was looking for. He was Aymelek's friend, and she thinks he might be dead.

Then I started a fire and sat by it, listening to the sounds outside to take my mind off the topic. It had started raining again, but I was not worried. I had prepared for the rainy season with enough food and firewood to last me a few days in my home. And I had an umbrella to keep me dry if I needed to go out.

It was still early, but the rain made me want to snuggle up in the blanket. The fire burned brightly and kept me warm. The soft, warm blanket around me felt comforting, even protective.

The sound of footsteps startled me. Someone was coming. I looked through the window and found a person carrying a lantern, walking toward my home. My mind played tricks on me and filled me with sudden fear. The evil wizard could be coming to steal my soul. My breathing grew faster. I tried to push back the irrational thought and kept my eyes on the person outside. Soon I recognized the visitor and was relieved to see that it was Aymelek. I opened the door to let her out of the rain. She left her umbrella on the side and asked if she could stay for the night. I was surprised and happy at the same time. The knowledge of a wizard living on the island was unsettling. I welcomed her company.

She made tea as we chatted casually, and then she came to the reason for her visit. "I heard you were looking for Qilam. Did you meet him?"

"Yes, I met him. He told me about Alfred," I responded.

"Listen, I don't want to tell you what you should or should not do. I just want to share some things that Alfred told me. He was my friend, and we talked about his conversations with Qilam in detail. I tried to stop him from leaving, but he had made up his mind. I'm worried that you are on the same path."

I quickly assured her, "Don't worry, I have no plans to leave the island."

She raised her eyebrows, "Well, that is great. Still, I want you to know that Qilam is not what he appears to be. Alfred told me how he urged him to think of different ways to leave the island. It was Qilam's idea to build a big boat. Alfred liked the idea, but it was Qilam who was behind it. He convinced Alfred to leave and look for another island past the Dark End."

"Hmm, Qilam made it sound like he was worried for Alfred, but Alfred still wanted to go," I added.

"That's not what happened. I want you to know that you can not trust anything Qilam says. He is full of lies. Did he talk to you about reading the poem literally?"

"Yes," I said. I was curious to see what Aymelek thought of it. Qilam had told me the villagers were lying, and now,

Aymelek was saying the same about him. Looking at her kind face, I hoped Qilam was the liar, not her. I liked her, and the thought that she could be deceiving me was more troubling.

She continued forcefully, "It's all nonsense! If gods wanted to send a literal instruction, why call the body a vessel? Why say it is sinking instead of dying? I don't mean to say that I have the answers. I'm just trying to point out that Qilam doesn't know either. No one knows. I have had these conversations with Alfred many times. I know how Qilam manipulates people into leaving the island. And I don't think Alfred is the only one. Since Qilam started talking about the mission to find more lands, four other people have left the island to Light-knows-what fate."

Aymelek spoke with such insistence that I felt she really cared for me. We stayed up late and chatted about other things, but Aymelek made it clear that the reason she came to see me was to protect and warn me.

I told her what Qilam said about the evil wizard.

She nodded, "Yes, that is correct, but the wizard hasn't been seen in a long time. The Seren think that he may have left the island, or maybe he is still here hiding and waiting for another victim to trap. The wizard and Qilam's words are equally dangerous. Both want to send people off the island to see what is next, and both are scared of trying it for themselves."

A chilling thought crossed my mind. Qilam said the wizard wanted others to try to go forward, and only when he is sure that it works, he will go forward himself. According to Aymelek, Qilam was the one who was convincing people to go on. I had heard him talking about it, and I had to admit he was pretty convinging.

"What if Qilam is the wizard?" I gave words to my thought in a shivering voice.

Aymelek laughed. "Honestly, I have thought the same thought so many times, but we have known Qilam all his life. He came before me, but people have seen him live among us since he came to the island in a boat. He is a coward and has the same ideas, but he is not evil. He hasn't hurt anyone except with his words. And the tree under the fall decided that he did not have magic, so he can't be the wizard."

"How does this test for magic work? Why is the tree used as a prison?" I had thought about this question so many times that I was surprised I hadn't asked it yet.

She explained, "The magic of the tree under the fall stops magical beings from leaving it. Anyone without magic can come and go freely. And it is a prison in the daytime only. At sunset, the barrier disappears, so we can not keep anyone imprisoned forever."

"But Feray has magic, and she can go in and out?" On the day of my arrival, I saw Feray enter the prison tree. It was still daytime, and Feray could leave freely.

Aymelek smiled proudly and said, "That's an excellent observation. Feray was able to enter and leave the tree because she was wearing a small Moonlight vial in her necklace."

"You are her apprentice. Does that mean you also have magic? What can you do?"

She smiled and said, "Yes, Feray and I can, for the lack of a better word, call the light. This ability is our magical power, and through it, we can capture and store it in a vial and then use the lights to heal others. We can not do any other magic."

We continued chatting late into the night. Aymelek told me that she was still learning to capture the lights. She was also very excited about a new project that Feray and Kratos were working on. I had heard Kratos and Idir mention it at the forge.

She had to go to work in the early morning, so we had to go to sleep. I slept on the rug in front of the stone fireplace and asked her to sleep in the bed. She hesitated but agreed when I insisted. This was the least I could do to repay her.

Chapter 5

I woke up the following day to find that Aymelek had already left for work. But before she left, she had prepared my breakfast and set it on the table. My day started with a smile at her kindness.

I thought about the reason for her visit. She wanted me to stay away from Qilam. Last night, I had already decided that I was too inexperienced to go looking for new islands.

Now I needed to find something else to think about. I remembered Fabio's question. He wanted to know a way to judge if he was doing the right job. This question didn't interest me much, and while I tried, I quickly got bored and decided I would think about it later.

The rain had stopped, but water still flowed over the steep wall of the hill, forming a temporary waterfall. The swamp had disappeared, and in its place was a pond. I was happy to be rid of the swamp, even if it was temporary, and wanted to enjoy the new landscape. I dragged the boat from the backyard and put it in the pond, then used a tree branch as an oar to move around in the water. It was so much fun.

I lay down in the boat and tried to remember how I must have been when I woke up near the dinosaur island. But there was not much to remember.

It wasn't too warm, and the sunlight felt good on my skin. The waves in the pond were small, but the boat still kept moving. The sound of the waterfall added to the relaxed atmosphere. I wanted to make the most of it before the pond turned back into a swamp, so I stayed on the boat for quite a while.

Lying in the boat and looking at the sky felt like a luxury. My empty mind kept going back to my work as a thinker. What was I supposed to think about? The only things that I had found interesting were dangerous. I had to meet more people and explore the island to find an interesting question to answer.

Why do we have wings but can't fly? The question flashed in my mind, and I decided to focus on it in the days to come. First, I needed to know what the people already knew about wings.

I closed my eyes and tried to imagine I was flying. The slight movements in the water gave my imagination a realistic touch. I felt like I was floating in the air. Small tremors ran through my shoulders as my wings ached to take flight.

Sometime after midday, I got out of the boat, tied it to a tree, and went to the village center for food. I questioned the cook about the wings. I was amazed to know that he had been practicing and he could hover in the air and cover small distances. He advised me to exercise my wings often so the muscles could grow strong and carry me in the air for longer.

Later, I met an old lady in the village center. She welcomed the question and gave quite a lengthy response. It was a story that she had heard in her childhood. She said there was a time when we could fly, but slowly, as we became lazy and preferred to stay on the land, we lost the ability. She thought, with some training, we should still be able to fly. With the shake of her head, she concluded soberly, "We have wings, but we don't fly."

After talking to a few more people, I realized that most believed that our lifestyle was too lazy; we did not exercise enough, which was why our wings could not carry us. But then I met another woman who had been very active all her life. She thought there was more to it. I wanted to hear her theory in detail.

She explained, "Look at the birds and animals. Most living things have so much in common with us; two eyes, one nose, one mouth, two ears, two arms, and two legs. Yes, there are differences, but why are we so similar?" She paused to let the question sink in, then continued, "I think people and animals started from the same thing. Whatever it was, that creature had two eyes, one nose, two ears, etc. Over time, we changed in different ways, and over a much longer time, we have become quite different. I think the creature that we started from had two arms, two legs, and two wings. Later, some of us lost our wings and became animals, yet others lost their arms and became birds. We kept arms and wings too. But as we became bigger and heavier, the wings could no longer carry us. I think, eventually, we will lose the wings entirely."

Another Seren explained that we were actually sons and daughters of gods. We had wings like gods and could fly around between heaven and land. But when we became mischievous and misbehaved, we were sent down to live on the ground as punishment. The gods ordered the wings to no longer carry us back to the heavens, so they remained with us only as a reminder that we should have behaved better.

The more stories I listened to, the more difficult it became to find the truth. It felt like a dead end, but I couldn't give up. I wanted to find an answer to at least one crucial question.

What good was a thinker who couldn't answer anything and just gave up? Of course, I understood that I wouldn't find the answers in a single day. It needed time.

I remembered what Feray had told me about the thinkers spending time in the yellow and green tree chambers. Maybe it was time to take help from the trees. I walked to the Tree Circle and entered the Yellowtree chamber.

Aymelek was sitting there quietly. Without disturbing her, I sat on the side and closed my eyes, just like her.

I sat quietly, waiting for the magical effect of the tree to do something. My focus was on my breathing and the question in my mind. Gradually, my head started to fall backward, and I fell asleep with an open mouth.

I dreamed about the creature that we started from - the one with arms, wings, and legs. The creature stood up, opened its arms, and spread its wings. A halo of light appeared right above its head as I realized it was a god. It looked at me angrily and sent me down to a land far beneath my feet. I protested, but it wouldn't listen. Once on land, I tried to flap my wings, but I could not fly. I cried out, but the cruel god was not there anymore—it would not help me.

I was alone in the tree chamber when I woke up. It was getting dark outside. I had lost track of time. I went to the village kitchen, picked some food, and headed home quickly.

It started to rain, and I was fully soaked when I reached home. I started a fire after changing my wet clothes and sat by it, thinking about the dream. I couldn't remember most of the details. I went to bed late that night.

The rain continued overnight, and I found the builder at my door in the morning. He had come to check if my home was in danger of flooding. The river had changed direction. The heavy rain overnight caused the water to overflow the river banks and change its path over the hill toward my swamp.

After a thorough inspection, the builder said, "Congratulations, your swamp problem is over. I believe the change in the direction of the river flow is permanent. The river will now flow over the hill in three waterfalls, each dropping into the swamp, turning it into a forever pond, but there is no danger to the house, as it is on raised ground. The overflow from the pond will go in a ditch that travels under the boardwalk and will meet the existing river, connecting back to it."

It was unbelievable. The swamp in my yard was replaced by a permanent pond and waterfalls. I had loved spending time in the water, and the prospect of doing it whenever I wanted was a fantastic surprise.

The surprises for the day were not over. The next one came with Idir. He came to talk to me about adopting a pet. I had never seen a pet in the village, so it surprised me. He said the pets were tiny and had to be kept inside the home at all times. Many people had pets, but I had never visited anyone, so I had never seen one.

I wasn't sure if I could take care of a pet, but Idir tried to convince me, saying it could be a great way to have company when I was alone. I was still unsure but agreed to visit the pet keeper. If I didn't want one, I could leave without adopting.

Idir and I walked to the pet keeper's house. It was full of glass boxes with different animals scurrying in them. All the animals were tiny, so small that I could carry them in the palm of my hand, and they were so cute that I wanted to adopt every single one of them.

The pet keeper said that these animals were too small to survive in the wild. I had to provide for all their needs. They didn't ask for much. Just some attention, regular feeding and cleaning routine, and a box inside the house provided enough for them to enjoy life.

It became tough to choose between them. Eventually, I narrowed down my search to only a handful of options.

Lenni the Llama had light brown fur. It was so small that it slept on the palm of my hand.

Ice Cream was an all-white dog with icy blue eyes and a fluffy tail.

A jaguar was playing in its tiny pond and was very active and fun to watch. I read the name tag on its box and smiled. It was named Patches.

Then there was a monkey named Monkey, a green-eyed owl named Twig, a kangaroo named Pouch, a parrot named Hush, a glass octopus named Sprinter, and a sheep named THE GOAT in all capitals.

The pet keeper was quite a character and made sure to find the most amusing names for his pets.

In the end, I couldn't decide which pet I wanted and decided to come back another day to make a selection. Idir and I laughed as we remembered what I had said earlier, that I wasn't sure if I wanted one. Now, I wanted many, but as the keeper had explained, it was a big commitment, and I should only pick the one I really cared for. The keeper preferred that we keep the adopted pets forever because they bonded with their owners.

I thanked Idir for bringing me to see the pets. He replied, "Thank Kratos—it was his idea."

I wanted to thank him in person and went to the forge with Idir.

Kratos had been friendly to me since I arrived, and I wanted to do something nice for him, but I didn't know what. He was hammering a piece of metal while his companions were laying out the finished parts in the yard.

I thanked him for the idea to adopt a pet and then asked directly, "I want to do something nice for you, but I don't know what I can do."

He smiled and said, "You are a thinker, and I have many questions that you can help me with."

I couldn't believe I'd be any use with my limited knowledge, but I said, "Yes, I would love to do that."

He moved away from his work, and we sat on the chairs outside. He said, "I have lived here for a long time, and I try to always do the right thing. I help people when I can, and I work hard at my job, but I am not sure if I am successful in life or not. How can I know?"

I looked at him with wide eyes as he finished. I had not expected such a question, and it reminded me of what Idir had asked earlier. These questions were very different from what I had hoped.

Kratos and Idir were much older than me. If they couldn't find an answer, how could I tell them?

Kratos watched me for a bit and said, "You don't have to think about it now. Tell me later when you have the answer."

I promised I would though I worried I may not be able to tell him something he didn't already know.

Kratos moved in his chair and settled comfortably. It was a good opportunity to ask some questions. I started with asking him about the watch on everyone's wrist.

"Why do we have a watch? What do you think?"

Kratos raised his wrist, looked at it, and replied, "We don't know."

I wanted more details, "Is it made of metal? Did you try to pry it open and see what is inside it? Maybe we can find something interesting."

"Many have. I have, too. It stopped when I removed the glass from the metal case. There is nothing inside it. Just an empty shell. I'm sorry, but I didn't find anything interesting to tell you."

"Hmm, okay," I said disappointedly.

Kratos continued, "The watch and the boat are very mysterious. We've tried to probe but found no clues."

"What is mysterious about the boat?"

"All the boats look exactly the same. We have put many boats together and inspected them in detail. To the smallest detail, all boats are identical clones and totally indistinguishable from others. It is so strange because we have never found two pieces of wood that look alike. There are always small differences. The lines formed by the wood grain, the position of the knots, etc., give each piece of wood a unique appearance. Whoever made these boats has otherworldly powers and is way more capable than us. Maybe they used magic to create them."

I was getting used to receiving strange information that provided no answers and raised more questions. I listened quietly.

Kratos asked, "Did you notice the round-ish sphere in front of the boat? What do you think it is for?"

I had never paid much attention to it, but I remembered that there was a ball-like thing at the front end of the boat. I thought about it for a little while and then answered, "It must be there to make it easy to hold the boat. To move it."

Kratos nodded. "Many think that. But, if you actually hold it to drag or move the boat, your hand will be sore in no time. It's not a sphere. There are flat sides on it with sharp lines. If someone so capable made it, why did they make it so uncomfortable to hold? Again, we don't know, but it could be a symbol or a clue. No way to know for sure."

I stayed quiet. Thinking about what it could be. Kratos added, "If you count the bottom where the ball connects to the boat, it has twenty-six flat sides. Just thought you should know. Maybe someday you will find out what it means."

Why twenty-six? Was there any significance to that? I asked, "Have you seen this number appear in any other place?"

Kratos shook his head.

I was a thinker. I was supposed to understand things that others couldn't. So far, I couldn't even come up with a new theory to explain something. Everything I could think of had already been thought of and proved useless. I thought I could try thinking about these things in the Yellowtree or Greentree. I might come up with something new. But then I remembered that I was not the first thinker here. Many must have tried that too. I asked Kratos, "Have the trees helped find any answers?"

He said soberly, "No. Many theories but nothing for sure."

I felt useless. I wanted to play a meaningful role in this world, but I didn't know how I could find a new answer. Everything had been thought about, and there were no clues to follow that could take me on a new line of thought. It felt hopeless. I wanted to be of some use. Maybe I could contribute in some other way. I asked, "Can I help around the forge? Is there anything I can do here?"

Kratos replied kindly, "You don't have to do that, but if you want, you can help others move the big pieces."

I thanked Kratos as he returned to his work. I joined Fabio and Misa and helped them move the heavier parts. Every now and then, they would start giggling at a joke the other made. I felt much better now that I was actually helping. They were always fun to be around and very easy to talk to. I told them about my dream in the Yellowtree chamber. They laughed, and Misa said, "The Yellowtree is the most fun of all the trees."

I told them I saw Aymelek sitting there, and suddenly their faces turned sober. I couldn't understand what was wrong, so I asked.

Misa replied as Fabio stood by with a solemn expression. "She is so sad. I wonder if she will ever go back to how she used to be."

"What do you mean?"

Fabio answered this time, "Aymelek had a friend, Alfred. While they had different jobs, we almost always found them together. They were the loudest and most fun people in all of the village. And they were always up to something adventurous."

I thought of Aymelek and was surprised that her image in my head did not match with what he was telling me. She had always been calm and composed. I just could not picture her as loud, fun, and adventurous.

Fabio continued, "Alfred used to call her Kaur because she was never afraid of anything."

"Kaur?" I asked.

Fabio replied, "Yes, Kaur, meaning the lioness. Kaur was a fearless woman who lived on this island long ago. It's an old story. She defended the residents of the island against a powerful wizard."

I nodded, and Fabio continued, "You know how most Seren stay in the village even though the island is so big? Aymelek and Alfred were not like that. They explored the farthest reaches of the land, always looking for a new experience."

"Then what happened?" I asked sadly.

"Qilam happened," Misa growled. "He became friends with Alfred and convinced him to explore the world beyond this island. Aymelek tried to stop him, but he left."

Fabio added, "And since then, Aymelek has changed into this new person. So grown-up-like, boring and serious."

Misa continued, "And it's not only that she is mad at Alfred for leaving, but she also blames herself for not going with him."

We stood there quietly for some time, shaking our heads in sadness.

Kratos's voice woke us up, and we returned to work.

I could not shake the image of a happy Aymelek from my head. I had always thought Fabio and Misa were fun and happy, but the way they described Aymelek and Alfred, it was something else. A very strong feeling of dislike for Qilam crept up in my mind.

When the work at the forge was finished, we gathered all the tools and placed them neatly inside. Idir invited me to join them in the Bluetree, where they often went to relax after a day of hard work. Fabio and Misa insisted, and I agreed. They promised that after dinner, they would walk me home.

My sad mood changed soon after I entered the blue chamber. I felt happy and at peace, as did my new friends. Idir narrated the story of our visit to the pet keeper. We laughed at how I didn't want to adopt a pet initially, and then I wanted to adopt so many after seeing the pets.

The more time I spent with friends, the happier and more connected to them I felt. It was a great feeling to be part of a group. I had always considered myself a newcomer. But slowly, I was becoming one of them.

My thoughts drifted to Aymelek again. I wondered how she felt after losing her friend. Remembering their story made me sad again.

Idir started singing and stole my attention. He was quite a performer—he sang many songs as Fabio, Misa, and I relaxed and listened quietly. His talent was awe-inspiring.

Fabio invited me to join them every evening or whenever I could. I promised that I would. I loved being with them.

I told them that I was having trouble at my thinking job, and Idir responded with a philosophical answer: "Thinkers don't have a day job. Your job will keep you busy even while you are resting aimlessly. There is a saying about thinkers: 'For ninety-nine out of a hundred days, a thinker appears to be doing nothing, then on the hundredth day, he surprises everyone with a mind-blowing discovery.' The ninety-nine days are hard on the thinker, but the hundredth day pays off."

Misa comforted me, "Don't worry too much. It takes time. For now, just enjoy life."

Fabio requested Idir to recite their favorite poem.

Idir asked knowingly, "A beautiful world?"

Misa replied, "Of course. What else?"

Idir smiled and was about to start when Fabio raised a finger, asking him to wait. Then he looked at me and said, "You are in for a treat. Listen to this poem."

I sat up attentively. Idir cleared his throat.

Misa yelled, "No! Stand up. Read it aloud. Like you always do."

I was very curious now. What was so special about this poem? Whatever it was, Idir had my full attention. He stood up and started.

"A beautiful world,

So fascinating!

Its colors and shapes,

Scents and sounds bewitching,

Its blueprint,

A master plan,

Or systems glitching!

Harmony and sameness,

Bring order and perfection,

Or difference is beauty,

And balance in friction.

Patterns repeating,

Very calculating,

Wonderfully symmetrical,

And yet deviating!

A beautiful world,

So fascinating!

From a seed,

To a tree,

Precious,

Yet carefree,

Does it matter if it grows?

Or, as a seedling, it goes?

Cruel! and indifferent,

Its methods, unabating.

A beautiful world,

So fascinating!

I found myself,

But is this reality?

There's more to me,

Or just an oddity?

An accidental circumstance,

Or a purposeful soul!

A longing in my heart,

Wants it to be more.

A meaningless existence,

Or to-God elevating!

A beautiful world,

So fascinating!

Looking for something,

In wanderings alone,

Disturbance in nothing,

To flesh and bone.

Head raised high,

My passion knows no limit,

The depths of the ocean,

Or a perilous summit!

Brave in my heart,

And at times, imitating.

A beautiful world,

So fascinating!

A desperate hope,

That I won't drown,

But troubles and doubts,

Do cut me down,

I cry and whine,

And carry a frown,

But only for a while,

And then turn around.

Painful,

And sad,

But also elating!

A beautiful world,

So fascinating!

What is the point?

Where am I going?

Coming to an end,

Or I am still growing?

I'm thinking it right,

Or in the wrong context?

Is there a stop,

Or always a next.

I'm looking for more,

But also, debating!

A beautiful world,

So fascinating!

The need to know,

Is part of my whole,

Blindly go on,

Without knowing the goal,

It keeps me moving,

Does it make sense?

In successes and failures,

And situations intense!

But every new find,

Is so exhilarating!

A beautiful world,

So fascinating!

Another world opens,

Behind every door;

A new possibility,

Gives rise to more.

I'm curious at heart,

And nothing to bore;

Excitement and misery,

Fact and lore,

All are essential,

And part of my core.

A blend,

Of contrasts,

Intriguing,

And captivating!

A beautiful world,

So fascinating!

Make my own path,

Or walk predetermined fate?

A part of me,

Questions every detail,

Yet other wants to just,

Believe in magic,

Not comprehend?

Blind faith can be tragic!

I have a reasoning mind,

Not logic negating.

A beautiful world,

So fascinating!

I will find all mysteries,

Uncover all truths!

Continue to strive,

Prosper and thrive!

As long as I can,

Struggle to survive!

Because last time I checked,

I am still alive!

I'm passionate,

Curious,

Meditating!

I'm scheming, creating, procrastinating!

Struggling, defeating, contemplating!

Always and forever,

In pursuit of your secrets;

I am!

Untiring.

And unrelenting!

My beautiful world,

So fascinating!"

As Idir finished, Fabio and Misa were on their feet - charged up and very enthusiastic. They clapped and cheered for Idir, who smiled, bowed his head dramatically, and sat back down.

There were a lot of questions raised in the poem, but when I heard the part where it said, 'I found myself,' I was stuck thinking about who this 'I' was who was talking about the beautiful world. One thing was clear, we have had the same questions for a very long time, and we still didn't have all the answers.

Around me, Fabio and Misa were still complimenting Idir. I looked at him and found him looking at me. I smiled and clapped my hands. His face lit up with a bright smile. We settled down to relax.

I recalled Fabio's question. I still hadn't found an answer to it. Maybe it was time to visit the Greentree, "I want to sit under the Greentree for a little while to think about something."

Misa laughed. "Looks like we won't have to wait for a hundred days!"

I left them, promising to come back in a bit, and went to the Greentree. Sitting in its chamber, I focused on the question: how can one know if their job is right for them?

Without thought, I closed my eyes and lifted my head up. The Greenlight started to take its effect. I experienced a clarity of mind that I had not yet felt. I kept thinking for a long time.

Idir shook my shoulders, and I returned to the tree chamber and opened my eyes.

I was surprised to realize what had happened. I didn't just

think about Fabio's question—I also had the answer to Kratos's. I was lost in thought and had a conversation inside my head. I was talking to myself, and as I thought about one thing, the other me checked the reasoning behind it and corrected me when I was wrong, then showed me a better logic. I accepted the new line of thought. The experience was so clear in my head that, unlike the dream under the Yellowtree, I fully understood and remembered it. I contemplated both questions with such a clear understanding that everything became simple and straightforward. It was very strange, and I felt like these thoughts were not my own, as if I was thinking using another mind; one that was way more capable, and had experienced so much more than me, and saw things so clearly. Was it the tree? Was I talking to the tree, and it was sharing its infinite wisdom with me? I didn't know how, but I had the answers I was looking for. I left with Idir to tell Fabio the answer to his question.

Fabio and Misa were waiting outside the tree, and we started walking to the village center. On our way, I addressed Fabio, "I know the answer to your question."

"Really? That was fast." Fabio wore an amused smile. "What is it?"

Misa and Idir also wanted to hear the answer, but first, they wanted to know the question. Fabio repeated it, and I started answering it: "When you go home after a day's work if you feel accomplished, you may be doing the right job. If you go to sleep thinking about the next exciting thing you will do at work, you may be in the right job."

Idir, Fabio, and Misa stayed quiet. I couldn't tell what they were thinking. Did they find my answer good or really silly? I waited with anxious anticipation to hear their thoughts.

Nobody said anything as we reached a table and sat down for dinner. We ate quietly, and I kept wondering if what I said made any sense and whether it was helpful.

Finally, Idir broke the silence and said in an excited tone, "I am definitely in the right job."

Fabio and Misa stayed quiet.

After dinner, we walked the trail around the glowing trees. We were not alone now. Many people were walking in groups and enjoying the cool night air. It was breezy, and the wind made a gentle swishing and howling noise as it passed through the nearby forest. The rustling of the leaves and the dancing, glowing vines of light trees made the atmosphere even more enchanting. It was a beautiful night, and the clear starry sky looked magnificent. It reminded me of the poem. It truly was a beautiful world, and I was bewitched by its beauty.

The waterfalls in front of my home were also beautiful, and my friends had not yet seen them. I wanted them to experience the beauty with their own eyes, so I told them about the pond and the falls. They were astonished at the exciting turn of events. I invited them to come and enjoy the pond some time, and they said they would after Feray's project was over.

It was strange that they didn't know what they were making. Idir said it was always like that with the healer's projects—there was an element of secrecy. She only shared the design of individual parts and never told more than what she thought was needed to build the components.

It was getting late, so we headed home. First, we walked to Idir's home. He invited me to visit him sometime. I promised I would. Misa and Fabio lived closer to my home, so they accompanied me all the way back before they left. They couldn't see the falls in the dark, but as we heard the sounds of the falling water, they raised their heads a little, and a smile appeared on their curious faces.

After they left, sitting in front of the fireplace, I kept thinking about my new friends. It was a long day. I pictured Aymelek and Alfred happily exploring the island, although I still couldn't imagine her being fun and loud.

I also thought about which pet I wanted. I had finally made up my mind before I went to sleep.

Chapter 6

I went to the forge in the morning to see if I could help with anything. Feray's project needed just a few more days to complete. There wasn't much to do for me, so I wandered around, looking at the odd shapes of the metal structures spread out in the clearing.

When I got tired, I sat under a shady tree and listened to the sound of the hammer striking the metal over and over again.

Kratos saw me and came to sit with me. After greeting me, he patted my back and said, "I have never felt so clearly that I am doing the right job."

I looked at him in surprise.

He explained, "Idir told me about your answer to Fabio, and I am very impressed."

I felt happy but then a little shy. I had the answer to his question too, but I wasn't confident enough to say it out loud.

"Did you also think of an answer to my question?" He said the words I was afraid of hearing and looked at me with such interest as if I was some wise old man who *knew* things.

He had liked my answer to Fabio's question, which encouraged me. I decided to tell him what I thought, even if there was a chance that he wouldn't think it was a smart answer.

"You are successful in life if you have people who respect you and care for you. You are successful if you can make time to be with those people. You are successful if you can sit back, relax, and enjoy the food you eat. You are successful if you can finish your work and still have the time to do other things that you like to do, and you are successful if you can go to bed with a clear conscience."

Kratos's face was full of surprise. He put his hand on my shoulder and said, "I have met thinkers before. The way you say things is so simple and easy to understand. Thank you!"

He got up and walked away, nodding in such a content way that I felt he truly liked my answer. I stood up happily, patted myself on the shoulder, and left for the village center for the midday meal.

I had only just started eating when the bells rang. I didn't know what it meant. I looked around, puzzled, and saw a group of guardians run toward the river. Soon after, Aymelek came out of the Tree Circle, running after the guardians with her notebook.

I followed her quickly as I realized what was happening. By the time I reached the river, the guardians had surrounded a newcomer. Another boat had arrived. This one carried a girl who looked around as perplexed as I was on my first day.

I watched them go through the same routine they had with me. The newcomer was taken to the prison tree under the fall and was left alone as everyone hid and waited to see if she would do something. She stayed inside the tree. Then, Feray tested her for magic. She did not have any abilities, either. In the end, Kratos welcomed her to Serenus and brought her to the village center.

The village center was busier than usual as she ate her first meal. She was greeted by the same lady and sent to stay at the same lodge as me. It was all standard practice. As she waited inside and wondered about the strange world, we prepared for the party outside. The next day, we surprised her outside the lodge. I remembered how I had walked between the two groups toward the seating area, nodding and thanking everyone. She was much more active, jumping around with excitement, her wings fluttering behind her, shaking people's hands. We were very different.

After the performance on the stage, a girl declared that the newcomer would be a material researcher. Later, I asked Aymelek what it meant, and she said, "The newcomer is very interested in how different things look and feel. When she was in the boat, holding the sides to keep her balance, she kept feeling the grains of wood with her fingers. Since then, she has wanted to know about all kinds of materials. She asked me questions about what the spears that the guardians pointed at her were made of. She was also very interested in the note on the bedside table and how it could be folded without breaking apart and the basket I carried her breakfast in. You know, that sort of stuff, so we think she will be good at studying materials."

I asked Aymelek about the reason behind surrounding a newcomer with armed guardians. I believed it to be a negative experience. She explained that it was all a tradition, and there was a reason for every step. Some newcomers had behaved aggressively in the past, so it was best to take precautions.

Aymelek agreed that many things could be improved, but changing the old ways was difficult. She reminded me of Feray's cold attitude the day I had arrived. I was surprised that she had felt it too. She said Kratos had talked to Feray, requesting that she be friendlier to newcomers.

There was no doubt that Aymelek liked her teacher. She tried to convince me that while the healer wasn't good with words, she was a good person and a great teacher. I understood what she meant. I felt the same when Feray had talked to me about her work and showed me the magical trees.

After the party, I left for home and decided to meet the newcomer in the next few days to help her understand and adjust to life on the island.

Once she had her own house, I went to her with some firewood and the essentials for preparing her own breakfast. She had already picked a name: Pari.

Pari asked me questions about what different things were made out of. She would point at an object, and I would tell her what materials were used to make it. She would listen intently and then point to the next thing.

Aymelek was right—Pari was obsessed with different materials and how each was used.

Pari and I spent many days together. Exploring her new world, showing her around. And in a few days, I felt that she was more sure of her role in this world than I ever was.

She had a long list of materials that she had learned about. She came across a calcite piece that looked like a dragon scale. It sat proudly on the mantle of the fireplace in her home. She could spend hours looking at it intently, studying it with her eyes, imagining all kinds of uses for the mineral.

One day, I took her to the forge and introduced her to my friends. She was thrilled to see how different metals were used to make things. As she went from station to station, watching the workers perform various tasks, I sat with Fabio and Misa. They laughed and said they liked the pet I had adopted and pointed to Pari. I smirked at their comment and explained that I had totally forgotten about a pet since I was busy showing Pari around. I told them I intended to adopt one soon.

Fabio revealed that the healer's project was finally finished, and a party was organized at the village center to celebrate the completion of the lengthy project. As the evening came, the metal forgers went through the pages of instructions from Feray and then put down their tools. The project was officially complete.

"Let's head to the village. The celebration will start soon," Kratos announced. I walked over to him and waited as the forge was cleaned and organized, ready for the next day.

The working men and women left in groups, chatting and laughing excitedly. Everyone looked happy.

I accompanied Pari, Kratos, and Idir back to the village center. Kratos explained that while their part of the job was finished, it was yet to be assembled. But that was to be done by Feray.

After the meal was over, we got up and rearranged the tables. All the furniture was carried to the yard's edge, making a wooden circle with the benches in front.

We sat down facing the clear space in the middle. It was getting dark, and some villagers lit torches to illuminate the atmosphere.

The celebration started with a slow song. Everyone joined in and sang in a deep, soft tone. The words were strange, but they had a strong effect on me. It sounded like they were paying tribute to someone or something.

I sat quietly, enjoying the peaceful experience. It was a perfect transition from the excitement and urgency of their day's work.

As the song ended, Kratos explained it to me. It was an ancient song and was, indeed, a tribute to everything that nourished us - sunlight, trees, rain, fruits, just about everything. It was a custom to express gratitude for every blessing before starting the celebrations.

After that, the party picked up. Many Seren men and women stood and sang beautiful songs.

The music came from the wooden instruments of the musicians sitting in the middle of the yard. Gradually, it changed into a merry, frolicking tune.

A group of people got up and started a mesmerizing dance.

In the beginning, they held hands and danced in a circle around the instruments. Then all at once, they spread their shimmery wings and took flight.

I was spellbound. It was the first time I had seen the Seren in the air. They looked so graceful as they hovered up together and danced in a circle above us. The audience clapped and cheered loudly, singing along happily. They ended the dance with a sudden plunge to the ground with their wings pinned back to their bodies. As they came closer to the ground, they opened their wings and hovered a foot or so above the ground. I trembled with excitement.

I was surprised to learn that, with some practice, our wings could carry us for more than just a hover. The dance moves were proof that the wings were more capable. I couldn't say they were flying; it was more like rising up in the air and performing some acrobatics, but even that was much more than I had expected.

After that, every song was accompanied by a breathtaking dance in the air. I caught Kratos glancing around. He was looking for someone. "What's the matter, Kratos? You were expecting someone?"

"Feray is not here." He frowned.

"She might be busy preparing for her part of the work."

"I don't think so. She wouldn't miss a celebration in the past. But then, she…." He trailed off.

Concern grew inside me. If Kratos was worried, it must be serious. "What is it? Do you think there might be a problem?"

He sighed and whispered his concern to keep it between us. "Feray is not herself. Lately, she has been acting differently. I don't know what, but something has changed. I should go talk to her."

He stood abruptly. Before he could leave, the song ended. Idir called for him to dance with him. Kratos looked conflicted, but he couldn't refuse an excited-looking Idir.

Kratos joined Idir in the dance, and the crowd cheered and whistled. He was very graceful in his dancing, while Idir was more energetic. They were compatible with each other even though their styles were quite different.

As the night grew darker, the celebration ended. Idir laughed loudly while recounting the performances of the people.

Everyone returned to their homes. Pari had already left with another Seren. I walked back alone, but I was not afraid of the dark this time.

In the morning, Qilam surprised me with a visit. After my conversation with Aymelek, I did not want to talk to him, but he had come to my home and was a guest. I couldn't be rude and tell him to leave, so I listened to what he had to say.

He had come with terrible news and a warning. He told me that someone was planning to attack the village and steal all the vials of light from the tree chambers. I asked him for more details, but he said that was all he knew.

He left in a hurry, and I wondered why he came to me with this news. I didn't know if Qilam was telling the truth, but the warning was so dire that I had to inform the village quickly.

I ran toward the village center, still thinking about who I would tell. I decided to go to Alev, but then I remembered that the guardians had only allowed us in after recognizing Kratos. It was better to inform Kratos, so I ran toward the forge.

I arrived out of breath and found Kratos having tea with his fellow workers. They were usually very busy with work, but now they were sitting like they had nothing to do.

Kratos asked me to sit down and catch my breath. When I calmed down, he demanded that I tell him what had happened. I started talking immediately, but they couldn't understand a word. I paused, took a few deep breaths, and started again: "Someone will attack the village and steal all the vials."

I told them how Qilam came to my home and delivered the warning. Everyone was shocked. At first, they didn't want to believe that Qilam was being honest. Their mistrust of his words was evident, but it was also not easy to ignore him. Kratos wanted to know how Qilam knew of it. I did not know that.

Everyone was uneasy, but Kratos was furious. "Qilam definitely knows more. Who told him someone would steal? How did he come to know of it? He is hiding something. And what kind of attack? We need to find out more information as soon as possible." He instructed everyone to keep the news to themselves before asking me to follow him, and we headed to the village center.

Once we arrived at Alev's house, Kratos asked me to tell her what had happened. I delivered the bad news. Her jaw dropped in disbelief. She called Boris and told him to increase the number of guardians around the trees, and then she called Feray. Her reaction was similar.

Kratos asked Alev if she thought it could be the wizard. She replied, "He has no accomplices. Since we started the tradition of giving a good experience, all the newcomers have stayed in the village and are accounted for. No one has joined him. I doubt he will try to do something like that himself. He will want an accomplice. It could be him but through another. We need to find out who is helping him. I suspect Qilam. We must arrest him immediately."

Feray and Kratos agreed as Alev decided that the matter should be kept a secret till more information was known. She asked me to keep quiet about it. Then ordered Boris to find and capture Qilam.

When we left, Feray was beyond herself. Kratos and I tried to calm her down. We understood that she was the one most affected by the news. It was her life's work that was at risk.

Kratos suggested that they would halt the work on the project till this mystery was resolved. Feray agreed. They wanted to focus all their attention on finding out whether it was true and how they could stop it from happening.

Before this day, I had only seen happy faces on the island. Now, it was different. Everyone was tense and afraid. Feray told Aymelek about Qilam's warning. She needed to know because of her involvement with the light and the magical trees.

A group of guardians passed by, running toward the Lighttrees. Everyone in the village center stood frozen, watching them.

We could keep the news a secret, but we could not hide the worry on our faces and the alarmed guardians protecting the trees.

Villagers figured out that something was wrong and started to whisper amongst themselves.

The only hope of getting more information was by finding Qilam. The day passed without any news of him. The guardians searched deep in the forest, but he was nowhere to be found.

I was at the forge with Idir when Feray arrived. It was evening. She was there to discuss her project with Kratos. Idir and I heard the entire conversation. She had changed her mind about delaying it.

Kratos disagreed with her. He believed that at the moment, it was better to not start something new and wait till things became clearer.

Feray insisted that her project was needed now more than ever before.

Kratos demanded to know the reason for urgency, but Feray wouldn't tell him. Their conversation ended in an argument, and she left furious.

I didn't understand why completing the project was so important at such a taxing time. I thought Aymelek would know the reason for Feray's insistence and decided to ask her.

I went to look for Aymelek in the tree chambers. The guardians stationed outside did not allow me in but informed that Aymelek was not there. I thought she might have left for her home already, but I wanted to be sure, so I went to check Feray's house before leaving for the village.

As I walked to the healer's house, I wondered if Feray would ever show me what was in the Moontree chamber.

I reached her house but stopped as I heard the voices coming from inside. Feray was arguing with someone. My instincts told me to hide. I went to the back of the house and stood by a window. The voices were low but still clear. A shrill, menacing voice traveled through the window.

"Have you lost your mind? We have come this far, and now you say you are not sure?"

Feray's voice was weak and tired. "I don't know if this is what I want."

I moved closer to the window to peek inside. An old lady with silvery-white hair stood in front of Feray. Her face betrayed her desperation.

"Of course, you do," the old lady insisted impatiently, then she walked away from Feray and stood by a table stacked with rolls of paper. The lady studied something on the table for some time. Then, she turned to Feray again. Her voice was calm and relaxed now and showed no hint of anger. "You are the most talented healer I have ever seen. I shared my knowledge with you because you showed so much potential. It would be silly to step back when greatness is just a step away."

Feray pulled herself together. The old lady's praise softened her tense face. She said in a firm tone, "I value your faith in me. You know I am grateful for all you have done for me. I feel troubled only because none of the healers before me have attempted such a thing."

The old lady laughed sweetly. "Oh! Now I understand what's happening. It is not you. It's the nerves. They create doubt in the heart of the one who is attempting something new, something exceptional." She patted Feray's shoulder and continued, "Now, now. Don't overthink. I promise you everything will go smoothly. You have a duty to your land. And only you can protect it. Remember! I believe in you."

The old lady was really good at encouraging Feray, who now stood stronger with a proud smile on her face. "You are right. I am so thankful for what you have done for me. I don't know how I will ever repay you."

The old lady patted her on the shoulder and said, "No need for such thoughts. Show the world what you are capable of, and surprise everyone. Do your duty... that's all I want!"

Feray smiled broadly, said she would check on the things she needed for the morning, and left. I waited to see where she was going. I didn't want her to see me hiding outside her house.

Feray walked to the Tree Circle and disappeared inside the Moontree. I wasn't sure what to do. I had no idea how long she would take in the white chamber, so I stayed where I was.

"Cursed place! When will I get out of here?" The old lady's voice was full of disgust. The sudden change in her tone shocked me. I peeked inside through the window.

She was tense and kept mumbling something inaudible. "Just one more night," she muttered slyly under her breath many times. Something strange was going on. I wondered what she meant by getting out of here. And what did she expect to happen after this one more night?

The more I thought, the more sinister the lady seemed. At first, she was patronizing in front of Feray and then had talked to her kindly but sounded cunning and deceitful when alone.

I remembered Feray's reluctance to let me inside her house. Was she hiding the old lady in her home? All kinds of doubts popped inside my head.

I couldn't understand what was happening there and whether Feray was doing something terrible. I decided to go back and tell Kratos, but I had to wait for Feray to come back. I couldn't risk getting caught. I was also worried that the guardians might tell Feray I had come to her home.

Confused and scared, I slumped down with my back to the wall and waited.

In a few moments, which felt like an eternity to me, Feray returned to her house. Without making a noise, I got up and peeked inside. She entered the room and stood by the table, studying the papers carefully as the old lady observed her. This was my chance to leave.

I snuck around the house with quick, careful steps. Without looking back, I crossed the yard and left. The guardians had seen me go to Feray's home and leave, but they had no reason to doubt my intentions.

I walked briskly to Aymelek's home and asked her to take me to Kratos. She saw the worried look on my face and led me to his place without question.

Kratos looked at Aymelek and me uneasily. He could sense that something was wrong. He let us into his dimly-lit home, and we sat down on a bench by the fireplace.

Kratos lit a torch, and I looked around. The home was the same size as mine. Some chairs were facing the simply-built stone fireplace, and a large table stood next to a wall with a raised bed.

Kratos looked at Aymelek, who was looking at me, waiting for me to say something. He turned to me and asked, "What happened?"

I whispered in response, "I have to tell you something important and strange. It might be nothing, but I have a bad feeling about it."

Kratos spoke in a kind voice, "Don't worry. Just tell me."

Aymelek watched me with a tense face. Kratos sensed my hesitation and said, "You are safe with us. There is nothing to worry about. Tell us what happened."

I recounted everything, starting with how I went to look for Aymelek to the conversation I overheard at the healer's house. Then I told them how the white-haired lady was full of disgust for this place and wanted to get out of here and that she thought she had to wait one more night.

Kratos's expression told me that I was right in thinking no

one knew about the old lady. He asked me to repeat the entire thing. I narrated the whole story again. He stood up and started pacing, deep in thought. His silence grew longer as I waited for him to say something.

Aymelek also stayed quiet, thinking.

I couldn't wait any longer. "What do you think is happening? Who is the old lady?"

Kratos spoke first: "I have never seen a white-haired lady in the village."

Aymelek added, "That's why Feray wouldn't let me in her home. What is she up to?"

Kratos sat down on a chair. "I don't know who the lady is. I don't think anyone knows about her. Feray has been hiding her from us. But why would she do that? They were probably talking about the project we were working on. It seems of great importance to Feray, and she argued with me earlier in the day, but she wouldn't tell me the purpose of the thing." He sighed and rubbed his head anxiously. "What are they up to?"

He stood up and started pacing again. Eventually, Kratos said, "You did a great job coming to me. Keep it to yourself for now. I will talk to Feray. I trust her. She may have a reason for what she is doing."

Aymelek nodded in agreement.

I was not happy with what they were saying. I didn't think there could be a reasonable explanation for Feray's actions.

Kratos saw the look on my face and said, "Whatever they

are doing is not happening tonight. I will go to her early in the morning and confront her."

We left Kratos's home, and Aymelek walked me back to mine. She was surprised to hear the sounds of the waterfalls and to find a pond in place of the swamp in my yard.

I was very uneasy with what I had witnessed. Aymelek offered to stay with me, and I readily accepted her offer.

We sat by the fire as she talked about how Feray had changed in the past few weeks. She was different and secretive and had lost interest in teaching Aymelek. All she cared about was being alone, and she constantly found reasons to send Aymelek away.

We also talked about Alfred. She was still sad about losing him and talked about their long walks and endless discussions on the trails.

Alfred was very passionate and wanted to be the best at everything he did. She told me about the wooden towers that people had built in the past in an attempt to spot a piece of land ahead. Alfred had constructed the tallest one. He didn't find another island, but they were happy to spend time looking at the beautiful world from the very top.

I asked, "If you could say one more thing to him, what would it be?"

She replied without a thought, "Don't leave… but if you must, take me with you."

"Why do you think he left?" I wondered.

"The lost scroll." She stopped abruptly and bent her head in embarrassment. Her expressions made me feel as if she had done something wrong.

"What is the lost scroll? I haven't heard anyone ever mention it."

Aymelek responded passively, "There is a story about some ancient knowledge that was lost forever. It is said that whoever finds it will become an all-powerful wizard. I think it's just another story made up by Seren in the past. Gradually, people started believing it to be the truth. Everyone wants to find the lost knowledge. It is why Alfred left; to look for it in the other lands. He believed that once he found it, he would become powerful enough to come back for me. Since the wizard has not been around for some time, we decided not to mention it to the newcomers. It is why everyone leaves the island. In search of unlimited power. I shouldn't have told you this."

"What kind of power does the scroll contain? Please tell me more." I could see that Aymelek wasn't willing to talk about this stuff, but my curiosity forced me to persuade.

Aymelek replied reluctantly, " Based on the story, which could be entirely false, the scroll contains knowledge so powerful that the owner of the scroll becomes a god and becomes free from all fears. It is said that this knowledge is so pure that it cannot be used for evil. But this doesn't stop people from looking for it for all kinds of selfish reasons. Alfred wanted to be the most powerful person in the world, but he wanted to do good things with his power. Unfortunately, most people think they are doing the right thing even when they are not."

Aymelek kept bringing the conversation back to Alfred. I understood that she missed him a lot and tried to comfort her and changed the topic to the falls.

I told her that the falls were now a permanent part of my front yard and shared my experience of being in my boat, listening to the sounds of the waterfall. She was excited to try it out herself.

She asked if she could sleep in the boat, listening to the sounds of the night and the falls. The sky was clear. I had no objection.

We managed to tie the boat so that it wouldn't move around at night. We connected both ends using loops that could be pulled on to move it to either end to get in or out. I went inside to my bed, and she slept in the boat, enjoying the starry sky above.

She wasn't afraid of the dark, and I could see why she and Alfred were good friends. They were both adventurers.

I was happy that I could offer her anxious mind some peace. I couldn't wait for the morning, so I went to sleep.

Chapter 7

Aymelek woke me up early, and we left for Kratos. He invited us to join him in a simple breakfast of bread and apricot jam. We ate together, and then Aymelek went to the healer's yard. She didn't want Feray to doubt anything.

Idir knocked at the door, and Kratos told him that he wanted to visit the Tree Circle, as he was feeling tired after days of continuous hard work. He promised to join us later, and we left for the forge.

While Idir kept talking to me, I couldn't concentrate on his words. My mind was preoccupied. Occasionally, I nodded to pretend I was listening.

The forge was full of people, busy working. They were repairing a cart used to carry firewood from the forest to the stockpile and a few other small jobs that were left pending while they were working on Feray's project.

Soon, Aymelek arrived with instructions from Feray to arrange the metal structures following her drawings. She had left as Kratos reached to talk to Feray.

Aymelek and I looked at the drawings curiously. I wanted to know what the final project would look like, but we were disappointed. The papers had no picture of the final product. It only showed how different parts came together.

Aymelek shared instructions with the workers at the forge, and they started to place pieces in their proper places.

As Aymelek supervised the workers, I stood under a shady tree with my back to the rough trunk. I watched absentmindedly as the scattered pieces started to form a shape.

As the last piece of the metal puzzle was carried closer to the almost solved figure, Idir joined me under the tree.

I had been thinking about Feray and Kratos constantly. What was happening there? Why did it take so long for Kratos to come? Was something wrong? There were too many what-ifs in my head, and every passing moment made me worry even more.

I made a conscious effort to divert my attention away from Kratos. I had seen Idir use his wings during the dance last night; I asked him if he had ever used them for longer flights.

"Let's just say that I don't use bridges to cross the river." He smiled, then continued more seriously, "We don't use the wings too often. They are delicate and precious. The most I have seen anyone fly is a few feet. We can glide much longer distances, though."

I nodded. "What if the wings get damaged? Can the healer fix them?"

"Yes, she can. That's where the Moonlight comes in. Aymelek must have told you about it."

She hadn't. In fact, I had not seen the Whitetree chamber.

Now I understood what was inside there. I asked Idir to tell me more about it.

"Well, I am not a healer. I might not explain it properly, but I understand that Moonlight is the most precious of all the lights. It's quite challenging to acquire in large quantities, as it is only available during a full moon. Moonlight falls on the moon-flowers, and the healer captures the reflected light. We keep the Moonlight safe and only use it when necessary."

"How is it used?"

"Among other things, the healers have a special power. They can manipulate the Moonlight. I have only seen it happen once." He paused as the workers dropped a piece with a loud bang.

Idir went to inspect the structure. After some moments, he came back satisfied, "No harm done."

"You were telling me how you saw Moonlight being used."

"Yes, right. So, one of the men fell off a tree during harvest time. His wing was badly injured. We carried him to the White-tree chamber. Feray put her hand in a vial full of Moonlight and brought it out as if it were a thread. She used some strange tools and built up the injured part all by herself. It was magic." Recalling the incredible event had lit up Idir's face. "The Moonlight is special. Everything that has the Moonlight threaded into it is alive. I have witnessed it. The wing of the poor man was as real as it could be. That is why it is so precious."

It was incredible. I thought about the magical Moonlight with wonder. Idir interrupted, asking if I would like an apricot. I said yes, and he pointed to the tree where the fruits hung.

He was about to climb when I stopped him and offered to do it. I wanted to take a look around from the top of the tree. Idir agreed.

Climbing the tree was easy. Once up, I glanced around and saw all the pieces of metal forming a familiar shape. I couldn't believe what I saw.

The metal structure had a long, thin body, narrowing down into a whip-like tail. Large wings spread on both sides. On the front was a head with a flat snout. Two holes in the head replaced the eyes.

I was terrified to see a metal creature, much like a dragon. It was too large to recognize from the ground. The workers walked around it without noticing what it was.

My mind worked fast as I quickly picked some apricots on my way back to the ground. I handed some to Idir. *Should I tell Idir? Or wait for Kratos to come?* I couldn't decide.

Feray arrived at the forge, pushing a wooden cart covered with a large cloth. Aymelek walked to her, and they started to inspect the metal creature.

Idir went to Feray to see if she needed help. They spoke for a bit, and then Feray continued the inspection of the parts. When she was satisfied, she announced that it was time for her to work and she needed everyone to leave her alone. "It would spoil the surprise," she insisted.

The workers left slowly. I kept my eyes on the path leading to the village. Kratos would be here any minute, I hoped.

Idir called me and pointed toward the village. He wanted me to leave. I walked over to him and asked about Kratos. Feray had told Idir she had finally convinced Kratos to let her proceed. She informed him that Kratos was feeling tired and was staying in the orange chamber but would be back soon.

Idir trusted Feray's word, and Kratos had also told him that he was feeling tired, so he had no reason to doubt her. But it frustrated me. I needed to talk to Kratos to see if he knew that he made a dragon.

I accompanied Idir back to the village center and sat there quietly, waiting for Kratos to come. The yard was noisy and busy. A large group of trainee forgers surrounded Idir, asking questions about the project. He was happy and went into a detailed description of the techniques they had used. I listened without any interest and kept glancing at the guardians stationed outside the trees.

The sun rose higher in the sky. The day turned into a pleasant one, white fluffy clouds floating in the blue sky. The cool breeze gradually picked up pace and scattered the delicate flowers fluttering off the trees. The beautiful scenery did nothing to calm me down.

I was drained from worrying about Kratos and the realization at the forge. I wanted to go see him immediately. I decided to try my luck with the guardians, hoping they would let me see Kratos.

"Idir! I'm going for a walk," I said and walked away. Idir nodded as he turned his attention back to his audience.

I headed to the Orangetree and asked the guardians if I could see Kratos. To my surprise, they said he wasn't there. I thought he might be in another chamber. I went to all the trees one after the other, but the guardians said the same thing every time. Kratos had not come to any tree. I began to panic. Why did Feray lie about him coming there? An unknown fear crept into my thoughts. Was Kratos in some kind of danger? I needed to find him immediately.

I went to look for him in Feray's home. Maybe he went to talk to the white-haired lady. Once there, I waited outside for a bit, wondering if the white-haired lady was inside. I didn't know if she could harm me if I encountered her.

A soft moaning sound came from inside. There was something wrong. I couldn't figure out who it was. The sound came again. I went forward, opened the door carefully, and gasped with horror. Kratos lay motionless on the floor. I rushed to his side and called his name, but he did not answer. He was unconscious. My mind was numb with fear and worry. I kept saying his name over and over again, but he remained unresponsive.

An idea flashed through my disoriented thoughts: I had to take Kratos to one of the tree chambers. Feray had told me the lights could heal the body and mind. He might recover if I quickly brought him to the right tree. I tried to remember. Redlight for ailments of blood, orange was good for.... I couldn't recall.

I tried to pull him up. He was very heavy, but I didn't stop. I kept trying, straining my muscles till I could bring him in a position where I could drag him along.

Once outside, I screamed at the top of my lungs for the guardians to come. They ran over, moved me aside, and carried him toward the trees. I followed along nervously. One of the guardians whistled, and more ran toward the healer's home.

I stayed with the guardians who were carrying Kratos to the Orangetree. They carried him inside the tree but didn't allow me inside.

I ran to get Aymelek and found her coming toward the village. As usual, Feray had told her to leave. I pulled her toward the Orangetree as I told her about Kratos.

She ran to the tree and disappeared inside as I waited outside with the guardians, my breath heavy from anxiety.

The guardians searched Feray's home, and the commotion of guardians' whistles attracted everyone in the village center. I found Idir looking at me and signaled him to come.

He ran past the guardians and reached me. "What happened?"

I was out of breath, and my legs could no longer carry me. I collapsed to the ground. Idir sat down with me and held my hand to comfort me. Finally, I found my voice.

I told Idir what had happened. As soon as he understood what I was saying, he ran toward the tree chamber, but the guardians held him back. He stood there, rubbing his hands uneasily.

Newly arrived guardians stopped more Seren from coming over to the trees. I waited patiently to hear some news from

Aymelek. Idir was also sitting on the ground now.

The guardians searching the healer's home had finished but did not find the old lady. They ran toward us and surrounded me.

Their commander came forward and asked me how I knew that Kratos needed help. I told him I had heard him moaning. He wasn't satisfied with my answer. He wanted to know why I was roaming around near the healer's house.

I said, "I was looking for Kratos. Idir told me he was resting in a tree chamber, but the guardians outside all chambers told me that he wasn't there, so I thought he might be at Feray's home." Idir nodded in agreement. The guardians backed away.

A loud swishing sound made everyone turn toward the village center. For a minute, everyone became quiet, trying to understand the sound. Then screams echoed through the village.

The peace of the day became a forgotten thing. Everyone ran around to get a clear view of what was happening.

As we exited the Tree Circle, I saw the frightful monster in the sky—the giant creature hovered high above the forge, flapping its wings slowly. I looked at it in horror as the screaming Seren started to run away.

I froze in terror. The monstrous creature stayed where it was, simply flapping its wings. Gold and silver scales covered it huge body, shimmering in the sunlight. Its long tail cut through the air with an angry swish.

Suddenly, the trees close to the monster caught fire. The

beast stooped low and caught the trunks of the burning trees with its iron claws. It pulled them out of the ground, and with a thrust of its long and powerful wings, it flew toward the village.

The villagers screamed in panic and ran in different directions to escape the imminent danger. I ran and took cover behind the healer's home but couldn't stop myself from peeking out to see what was going on. The guardians ran toward the forge and whistled for more guardians to come. The bell in the village center was ringing, announcing the threat.

The burning trees came like arrows to the village. Wooden houses provided fuel to the eager flames, and they spread around, eating everything they could find.

More and more guardians appeared and shot arrows at the beast, but with a quick flap of its wings, the villain flew away, leaving its fiery army behind to devour the village.

The past few moments had changed the peaceful village center into a warzone. I rushed toward the magical trees to see if everyone was safe. There were still guardians outside. They had not left their stations.

Then, I ran to the village where the burning trees had fallen. A large tree was sprawled over an unfortunate house. Its branches spread all over the front garden while the thick roots stretched toward the sky like a bony hand. Then, with a loud noise, the roof collapsed under the weight of the tree.

I looked around with a numb feeling. The beautiful village was broken, burnt, and wasted all around me. It was unrecognizable. The wooden furniture in the village center was on fire.

Black smoke rose from the burning houses around it. It must have been late afternoon, but the sky turned dark with smoke and grey clouds that blocked the sunlight. A storm was coming.

A deafening silence echoed through the village amid the shuffling of running steps and the urgent words of the people trying frantically to put out the fire. But the flames were angry. Hungry, they wanted to eat everything they could reach.

The flames licked at the house next to me. The heat was too much. I moved away from it, keeping my eyes on the ground.

The smoke rising from every side made it difficult to breathe. The cough hurt my lungs, and I sat down, hugging myself tightly.

Then, I saw someone running toward the village center. It was Idir. I shouted loudly to let him know where I was. We ran toward each other, and I looked at him, waiting to hear about Kratos. His face told the story of the horror that surrounded us, but he was relieved to find me safe.

Idir wanted me to go with him. I followed quickly and without question. As we walked away from the burning village center, I kept looking around in disbelief. It was unbelievable how much destruction had taken place in such a short time.

The healer's yard was full of people. Many wooden cots had materialized, carrying the injured being taken to the chambers by the lucky survivors. We threaded our way through the groups of men and women standing together with empty eyes. They kept looking around nervously.

I was worried about Kratos and couldn't wait any longer.

"Idir! How is Kratos?"

Idir's words were full of worry. "Aymelek has moved him to the Moontree chamber. No one is allowed to see him."

He took me to the Redtree. Aymelek was already there, busy with some injured people. As we stood there, more and more wooden cots appeared. A girl was helping Aymelek. An assortment of jars with powders and liquids of different colors filled the tabletops.

It was getting crowded. Aymelek announced that everyone not injured should go to the Bluetree. Her helper informed her that it was already full. Villagers were agitated and needed to calm their minds.

Aymelek said loudly, "If you are not hurt, go to the Greentree. The Greenlight will soothe your senses. I will be there shortly."

I left with Idir and a few others for the Greentree. Boris was walking to Feray's house with more guardians. They looked alert, moving slowly. I wondered if they had found the old lady.

Idir pushed back the green curtain to let me in. Some people were sitting inside, but there was plenty of room here. No one looked up as we entered. We found a quiet corner and sank to the ground side by side with our backs to a thick trunk carrying the green ceiling.

I watched as the cool Greenlight washed over me. It gently touched my mind, soothing it. I was on edge and looking around frantically, but the light had started to work its magic. I closed my eyes, took a few deep breaths, and felt my head become lighter, more focused.

After a few moments, I opened my eyes and looked around with a fresher mind. Idir was also looking better. I closed my eyes again.

It seemed like a lifetime had passed since Feray stood there with me, excitedly talking about how the Greenlight provided clarity to an anxious mind.

After all, it is nature's most preferred color. She had turned around to smile at me. I shook her image from my mind. I didn›t want to think about her, not after what she›d done.

The cracking of thunder brought me back. Aymelek was there with us. I had not seen her come in. I asked, "Aymelek, how is Kratos?"

"I am not sure. Kratos is not injured. Nothing is broken. But he is still unconscious. I have tried everything I know, but nothing worked. We are keeping him in the Moontree. But we need to figure out what happened." She turned toward Idir. "I need your help. Since Feray is not…." She stopped in mid-sentence. Her eyes started to fill with tears, and she rubbed them off with her hand. "Idir! Please go and bring Alev here. She might be able to help us."

Idir left quickly. Aymelek sat down on a bench and rubbed her forehead slowly. She was tired. I let her rest and sat on the bench next to her. She looked at me after a while and said softly, "I am so glad you went after Kratos. Whatever happened to him affected his heart. The Orangelight gave him strength and kept his body warm. You may have saved his life."

I nodded and hoped she was right. Aymelek left to check on the injured. Idir hadn't returned yet. The waiting would have been vicious if I hadn't been in the chamber lit in dim green. I put my head down on the table and closed my eyes. It felt good.

Footsteps approached me, and I slowly looked up. It was Boris, the head guardian. "You are needed at the healer's house. Come with me," he said soberly.

Outside the chamber, it was already dark, with the grey clouds taking over the blue sky. The fire burned brightly in the tall torches erected all around the yard. The air smelled of smoke, and a glance toward the village revealed the source. Boris told me that the fires had been put out. Some people were injured, and others were shocked, but no one had died.

The yard was almost deserted now. I followed Boris to the healer's house. Once inside, I saw an elderly man sitting in a chair beside Alev, who sat with a blanket covering her legs.

Idir sat on one side. Boris offered me a chair next to Idir and pulled himself one too.

I sat nervously under the steady gaze of the elders. Alev started, "This meeting has been called to make sense of the incident. Idir considers you to be innocent. We believe his word but can't leave anything to chance. I have to ask you to go through the details of how you came to find Kratos."

I told them everything I had told Kratos the previous night, and then about how I found him in the healer's home. Idir was in shock, as he knew none of it. The elders noticed it, and Alev demanded proof that I was telling the truth. I told them that Aymelek was with me last night when I went to tell Kratos about the white-haired lady.

Boris left to get Aymelek, and I noticed the burning stare from Idir. He was disappointed in me. He had trusted me, but I had kept everything from him. We were together all day, yet I revealed nothing. I tried to explain myself, "Kratos asked me not to tell anyone."

Idir crossed his arms and looked away.

Aymelek arrived, and the elders asked her to tell them about last night's meeting at Kratos's home. She narrated the same story that I had told them.

The elders asked more questions, and we responded honestly. When they were satisfied, Alev demanded that I repeat the conversation between Feray and the old lady. I told them all I knew. They sat silently, brooding over what I had told them.

The older man asked Alev to voice her opinion. She answered in a gruff voice, "Jinyan, I am afraid it must be Esmeray trying to achieve what she couldn't the last time."

Everyone gasped in horror. The room's atmosphere changed. Its grim, sad tone turned into one vibrating with anxiety. The elders exchanged glances and started whispering urgently amongst themselves.

Chapter 8

Idir cleared his throat loudly. "Who exactly is Esmeray? I know a bit of the story, but it doesn't make any sense."

"That's because no one knows the whole story," Alev explained.

Jinyan nodded gravely and said, "Esmeray was one of the best healers we ever had. She made brews and potions unlike any we had seen before. But she was very ambitious and wanted to use the magic of trees for her own selfish reasons. We don't know exactly what she wanted to do. She had us fooled with her charming ways; everyone except for Xahene, who figured out her intentions were not good. He tried to warn us, but we were under her spell. Esmeray attacked him when he stopped her from misusing the lights. They both died in the fight. Or so we thought. She was never seen again after the attack on Xahene."

Alev concluded, "If it really is Esmeray, we need to find the answers to two questions. What does she intend to do, and how did Xahene stop her the last time?"

The elders' meeting continued, but Idir, Aymelek, and I were told to leave. Aymelek returned to attend to the injured. Idir and I went toward our homes to pass the ill-fated night.

I asked Idir if he was still mad at me. He replied honestly, "I would have preferred that you told me once Feray lied to me, but I understand you were obeying Kratos."

"I didn't know Feray was capable of hurting him." I clarified.

He knew what I meant. Everyone was shocked by her actions.

"Why did Aymelek need Alev?" I asked.

"She is the old healer. The one before Feray. In fact, she taught Feray. Old age is cruel. Her hands started to tremble badly, and it got so bad that working with the lights was impossible. Then one day, the power to manipulate the Moonlight left her entirely. Feray has been the healer ever since."

We fell silent. Talking about Feray was not comfortable anymore. I had not known her for long. She came across as a proud person during most of our interactions, except when she talked about her work. I had actually liked that side of her personality. But it was different for everyone else. They had known, respected, and trusted her. Now that she had betrayed them, even saying her name was agonizing. Their wounds were fresh and raw.

Idir left for his home, and I continued on to my own. It was a terrible night. The storm had arrived, accompanied by the angry crackling of lightning. The air shook as the thunder growled and the angry rain beat the windows frantically. I pulled my blanket around me tightly and fell into a fitful sleep, dreaming about fire-spitting monsters and dark, mysterious places.

Early the next morning, I went to the village center to see how Kratos was doing. I still couldn't see him, but the guardians told me he was awake.

The village center was in ruins. The storm was long gone but had left puddles of water everywhere. I joined a large group of Seren who were clearing the rubble.

After a while, I saw a crowd started to gather in front of the elder's house. I joined them. The guardians told us that Feray had been captured late last night and Alev wanted the villagers to gather for an update on the situation.

Once everyone gathered, Alev spoke to the crowd, "Last night, Esmeray attacked the village."

The crowd gasped. Whispers echoed amongst them.

"This is what we know so far: Esmeray tricked Feray into helping her make that monster, and once she had it, she tried to kill Feray. Esmeray knew that Feray could stop her with her powers to manipulate light. We are lucky Feray escaped the fire, and the guardians found her. She is being held for further investigation, and we will share all the findings with everyone. Until then, our focus will be on protecting the village from further attacks. Rest assured that we are doing our best to prevent further damage and rebuild as fast as possible. We will gather again when we know more." Alev left, and the crowd started whispering in anxious disbelief.

I walked toward the Tree Circle to find Aymelek in the Redtree. I waited outside, and when she came out, inquired about Kratos. She led me to the Moontree in the middle of the Tree Circle.

This was the first time I had entered the Moontree. It was much larger than the others. Its chamber was more spacious, and the fruit bulb in the middle was massive.

I found Kratos on a bed right next to the bulb, awake.

Aymelek and I asked him how he was feeling. He looked weak but smiled at me and said, "Much better. You saved my life. I can't thank you enough."

I smiled back. "Don't worry about that. Just get better."

Aymelek briefed Kratos about the situation, "The elders think Feray is telling the truth. Esmeray tricked her into making the beast. They believe Feray did not intend for anyone to get hurt, and once she found out what Esmeray really wanted, she tried to stop her. Esmeray attacked Feray with a fireball, but she was lucky to survive. Guardians found her late at night, and now the elders are holding her to investigate further."

Kratos asked in clear frustration, "What does Esmeray want?"

Aymelek replied, "Based on what Feray has said, it appears Esmeray wanted to steal all the vials of light to keep her beast strong. After Qilam's warning, the guardians were placed to protect the trees. Therefore, Esmeray couldn't get the chance to steal the vials. We believe she will try again with her newfound weapon."

Kratos sighed. "Feray knew of this plan?"

Aymelek replied quickly, "No. Only now she is putting it all together. She thought she was building a guardian to protect the village against the evil wizard. Esmeray tricked Feray into thinking that this was the only chance that the village had against the wizard's upcoming attack."

"Esmeray is working with the wizard?" I asked.

"Well, we think Esmeray is the wizard," Aymelek said. "Or she is under his control. We don't know what it is, but the elders think Esmeray is the wizard who wanted to attack the village and steal the light."

Kratos asked, "What happens next? Where did she go after attacking the village? Do we know anything?"

Aymelek responded in a stern voice, "Everyone thinks she will come back. If she wants the vials, she will take them by force. It's just a matter of time."

We looked at each other with anxiety and fell silent. Aymelek was deep in thought while she fidgeted with her rings.

Idir entered the chamber and stopped when he saw our worried faces. Kratos asked him about Feray. He informed us that Feray was here in the Tree Circle, and it was decided that she would be tested by the Mirror. Kratos sighed, and Aymelek shook her head.

"What does that mean?" I asked.

"You will see. Let's go outside." Aymelek tried to stop Kratos as he needed to rest, but he got up slowly. Idir gave him his shoulder to lean on. With slow steps, they walked out of the Moontree chamber. Aymelek and I followed.

It looked like the entire village was gathered in the Tree Circle. I saw Feray sitting alone, halfway between the arch and the Moontree, and in the arch sat Alev with an old lady I didn't recognize. We went and stood next to the elders.

Feray was on her knees, sobbing like the one who had lost everything. She was holding a vial of white Moonlight in her hand. Her head was bowed. The Tree Circle was in complete silence except for her regretful sobs. The mourning echoed back from the rigid walls of the audience. Most of them had averted their eyes from the unfortunate woman they had respected so much. I looked at their faces, trying to understand what was happening here.

Aymelek stood next to a tense Idir, staring down at her feet. Tears ran down her cheeks silently. She kept wiping them off.

Everyone was angry with Feray, yet it was painful to see her in this state. We didn't know what we could do to end it, so we just stood there and heard her wail.

Alev welcomed Kratos and said, "I am happy to see that you are alright. If something were to happen to you…."

Feray sobbed and broke down into hysterics.

Alev looked at me and said, "You saved Kratos's life. Accept our gratitude… what is your name?"

"I have not picked a name yet," I responded meekly.

"Picking a name isn't that hard," Alev reprimanded.

"I am not yet sure what name will suit me." I felt the eyes of the entire village on me.

Alev shrugged dismissively, "You thinkers overthink everything."

Then Alev walked to Feray. She extended her trembling hands and took the vial from Feray's hand. Aymelek walked over and took the vial from Alev. The Moonlight vial started to glow brightly, bathing the surrounding in white light. I looked at Aymelek's face as if in a trance. She looked like an angel carrying a full moon in her hand. Feray's sobbing intensified.

Alev spoke sternly, "The Moonlight has rejected you. It has started to glow for Aymelek. Now, she is the Seren healer. The magic itself has made its decision."

Alev looked at the old lady, then back at Feray and said, "It is time, to tell the truth, Feray!"

Feray shook her head fiercely. "No, no… not yet. Let me explain. At least… please, give me a chance."

"Then tell us what you have to say for yourself. Why would you do such a thing?" Alev said.

The village waited quietly as Feray caught her breath and calmed herself down. Then, she recounted the events that led to the devastation Serenus had gone through.

"I was out in the forest one day. That place is rarely visited. I was looking for some mushrooms and herbs for making medicines. There were plenty, and I was busy collecting them when someone approached me. It was an old lady limping badly."

Feray sighed, shook her head, and continued in a coarse voice, "I left my things and helped her sit against a tree trunk. I had never seen her before. It was strange, as everyone here knows each other. I expressed my surprise, and she said that I was right. That we had never met before. She told me that her name was Savita, and she had been a healer before Alev. I had heard the name, so I thought she was telling the truth. I asked her why she wandered in the forest and did not live in the village. She told me the story of how she had been captured by the wizard, and the people thought she was dead. She stayed in captivity for a long time, and during her time with the wizard, she figured out his plans to attack the village. She said she had just escaped the wizard and came to warn us. I was foolish. I believed her words. Her old age made me think that she could not be a threat. She said she had a plan to defeat the wizard: by creating a powerful creature to fight him off. I trusted her. She asked me to keep her hidden so the wizard wouldn't know she had escaped. I thought it made sense."

Alev interrupted her story, "You thought Esmeray was Savita, my teacher? And you never thought to ask me about it? Savita died in front of my eyes. If you had talked to me, we would have found out that it was actually Esmeray."

Feray sighed and continued, "I see now that I was wrong. But at the time, I thought I was doing the right thing. I had no reason to doubt that she was not Savita. She taught me things that only an expert healer could know."

"Esmeray tricked you into creating a weapon for her. What does she intend to do next?" Alev asked.

Feray replied, "When we heard the warning from Qilam, I thought the attack was imminent, and so I helped her, putting aside all the concerns I had. I thought I was protecting everyone."

"What does Esmeray intend to do?" Alev repeated.

"I now believe that she lied about an attack from the wizard. She wanted the weapon for herself."

The villagers gasped loudly.

Feray continued, "Esmeray needs the vials of light to keep the creature alive and strong, and that is why she will attack the Tree Circle with her beast."

Everyone tensed, hearing about the possibility of another attack. The elders whispered amongst themselves.

Feray started sobbing again. Then, finally, she got hold of herself and spoke again. Her voice was teary. "I was stupid enough to believe her. She tricked me, and I fell for it. I brought her here with the best intention. She provided me with detailed illustrations. Kratos and others trusted me and followed my directions. If only I had known…."

Alev was stern. She was not going to show any kindness to Feray. "But you did, didn't you? You know the laws of Seren magic. Our magic is not to be used to create such a creature. It is unforgivable. Moreover, you defied the laws by keeping her hidden. You were supposed to inform the elders no matter what you thought or believed." She continued harshly, "I have known you since you were young. I know how ambitious you are. I taught you humility when you craved recognition and praise. But you didn't learn to subdue your desires. Don't act as if you never knew what you were doing. You did. You wanted to do something others couldn't. You were proud."

Feray's bowed head said it all. She knew the laws, yet she chose to perform the unspeakable act.

Jinyan, the elder sitting next to Alev, was equally strict. "Kratos came to talk to you. How do you explain what you did to him?"

"I didn't do anything. It was Esmeray. She didn't want him to mess up our plans. She said he would stay unconscious long enough to finish our work. I meant him no harm." Then Feray looked at me and continued, "You saved Kratos. I am in your debt forever. If something happened to him, I could never forgive myself."

Jinyan interjected, "What about the ones who got hurt in the attack? Have you forgiven yourself for inflicting misery on them?"

Feray continued with a bowed head, "I never meant any of it to happen. I thought I was protecting everyone."

Alev looked at the elder I had not met before. Her light blue eyes made her look different from others.

Alev said, "Alia, are you ready to test Feray?"

Feray sobbed as Alia replied in a cold, distant voice, "I am." She stood up slowly.

Boris signaled for everyone to sit down, and they moved away from Alia, leaving her alone in the middle of the arch.

Alia sat down on the ground under the arch.

Aymelek walked over to the Moontree and picked a white flower. She put it inside the Moonlight vial, and it started to move around ferociously, creating a bubbling mist.

Aymelek placed the vial in front of Alia. Her eyes were closed as though deep in meditation. Slowly, Moonlight started to calm down and glowed gently on Alia's face, giving her an outlandish look. Her expression was calm and graceful.

We waited quietly. I was curious about the trial. How were the elders going to judge Feray? It seemed impossible without any witnesses.

After some time, Alia opened her eyes and said, "I am ready. Bring her close."

Feray raised her head and looked at Alia, then addressed Alev angrily, "How can you do this to me? I have spent all my life here among my people. I have made one mistake, just one! And you are going to test me? Have you forgotten all that I have done?"

Alev stayed quiet, but her expression said it all. She didn't trust Feray.

Aymelek asked Feray to go ahead and sit by Alia. She lashed out at her. "I won't take this insult. I refuse to be tested." She turned and tried to walk away, but the guardians stopped her, holding her arms firmly. She resisted, but they did not let go.

Kratos went to Feray to try to calm her down. "Feray! Don't be difficult! No one is trying to insult you. We just want to be sure. It is better for you. Once your innocence is proved, no one will ever point the finger at you."

Kratos's words made it clear that he trusted Feray and believed she had unintentionally made a mistake.

Feray kept looking at Kratos with fear in her eyes like a bird in a cage, fluttering around anxiously with no hope of getting out. She pleaded, "Kratos! You are my friend. You know me. Don't let them do this to me."

Kratos consoled her, "There is nothing to worry about, Feray. You know you are innocent, then why are you worried? Go on. Sit with Alia!"

Feray shouted at him, trying to push the guardians away. "I can see what you are trying to do. You are no friend of mine." She looked around at the elders. "I don't accept this."

With a seething look at Kratos, she tried to break free, but the guardians were too strong. Boris asked them to take her forward. She kept resisting as they dragged her to Alia and tried to make her sit next to her. She shouted at them to leave her alone and fought with all her might. Kratos kept trying to calm her down. But she was senseless with anger.

It was difficult for the guardians to control her. Aymelek walked to the Bluetree and brought two more vials. One was blue, and the other was indigo. She put her hand in the blue vial and removed a strand of light. Then, she took a strand from the indigo vial and twisted the two strands together to form a rope. She combined the ends, and the lights merged to form a glowing crown.

Kratos and Boris helped the struggling guardians hold Feray down while Aymelek put the crown around her head. Her anguished expression slowly mellowed, and she stopped resisting. Her eyes softened, and she stared into space. Kratos and Boris helped her sit down in front of Alia and put her hands on the vial.

Alia put her hands on Feray's. The crowd became very silent in anticipation.

A bright yellow flame erupted above the Moonlight vial and flickered in a non-existent wind. I sensed an alien emotion but couldn't understand it enough to name it.

Slowly, the flame turned orange. It spread an uncomfortable ambiance around us. I looked at others to see if they had felt the change. They had. I turned my attention to Alia and was shocked to see her expression. She looked angry.

The flame quickly deepened into a red one. It burnt furiously, creating an eerie atmosphere. I felt the heat and was bothered by it. I became angry with it for being there. The feeling rushed through my veins and spread everywhere. Every passing moment fueled my anger. I was furious with everyone and everything. The intensity of the emotion shook me. I clenched my hands into fists.

I looked around the chamber, and my eyes rested on Aymelek. I realized that she was the reason for my anger. I hated her for having what I couldn't have. She didn't deserve the treasure she possessed. Only I was the one worthy of it. She had snatched it from me. The injustice increased my fury.

The flames turned into a roaring fire, and I heard Alia sneer at Aymelek. I realized that it was not just me. Everyone was furious with her. Though not as much as me. I loathed her beyond words.

I searched for Alev and found her sitting pompously in her

chair. Who did she think she was to decide for others? She must have been jealous of my achievements. I smirked with disgust. She could only dream of the power and intellect I had. The more I looked at her old wrinkled face, the angrier I became. It was unbearable to take her snobbishness anymore. I wanted to hurt her. I clenched my fists even tighter and felt my nails digging into my palms. I growled, and with a leap, I lunged at her, seething with anger. Strong hands pulled me back as I struggled to break free and attack her. I screamed uncontrollably as someone forced me down to the ground and held me there. I kicked and punched wherever I could, but they wouldn't let me free. The rage grew inside me till I felt that my body wouldn't take it anymore. Then, it stopped suddenly and started to subdue.

I slumped down to the ground. Slowly, my anger transformed into an emotion I couldn't understand. I trembled violently in its claws. I looked at the faces around me helplessly. None of them could help me. Behind them, the fire burned blue above the white orb. My heart ached, looking at the pure white light. The anger drained out of my body. Instead, I drowned in raw pain. What had I done? I wished time could go back. I wouldn't think of it ever again. NEVER! But the time had gone. There was nothing I could do. I wrapped my arms around my legs and rocked back and forth in hopeless agony. My face was drenched with tears. Why did I do it? What for? No answer came forth. I couldn't breathe. The air was suffocating me. I looked around in exasperation and saw my pain reflected on the desolate faces around me. Tears ran down their flushed cheeks. A sob escaped my mouth. The white orb with blue fire danced in front of my eyes as I slid down to the ground. The sobbing rocked my body. And my mind went dark.

I felt weak and tired as I opened my eyes and saw the flickering light from a torch lighting the dim room. I could see the room's wooden ceiling while lying on a bed. The place was familiar. I tried to remember where I was. My mind was clouded. How did I get here? It took me a long time to recover an image inside my head—a furious fire burning above a softly glowing white orb.

I remembered everything and felt sick. What had happened?

I recalled feeling jealous of Aymelek and was confused. I had always liked her, but earlier, I wanted to hurt her. I was furious at everyone in Serenus. I felt cheated out of my fair right. Then, I had tried to attack Alev. The memory of it shocked me. What was it that came afterward? An emotion that was so strong and painful that my mind couldn't take it, and I had fallen unconscious. There was no reason for me to feel what I had. Yet I felt it deeply.

The door opened, and Kratos entered the room. His face was drawn and tired. But he was relieved to see me.

"Thank the Light! You are awake. We were worried about you. How are you feeling now?"

He sat next to me and watched me with concerned eyes.

"Tired, but fine," I said.

He sighed in relief.

"Kratos! What happened to me? I attacked Alev!" I asked him. My desperate voice betrayed my feelings of shock and shame.

He watched me with kindness and said, "What do you think happened to you?"

I went over the memories again, trying to find the reason for the incredible experience. There was no reason to feel the way I did. I knew those emotions were not mine. They couldn't be. If anyone could feel that way... it was Feray.

"Did I feel what Feray was feeling? Jealous of Aymelek for taking her place. Proud of her own talent and angered by Alev's decision to test her."

Kratos nodded. He looked sad and tired too. "That's right. You felt what Feray was feeling at the time. At first, I was surprised by her resistance because I believed with all my heart that she was innocent. But now, it is clear that she wasn't. She helped Esmeray because she was too proud of herself and wanted to do something no one had ever done without regard to right and wrong. She was jealous of Aymelek and hated her. You attacking Alev was, in fact, a reflection of the hatred Feray felt toward her."

He paused and sighed loudly. I felt sad for him. He had believed in Feray and truly cared for her, but she had let him down. It was not easy to deal with such a blow.

"I am sorry, Kratos. I know how you must be feeling."

He gave a slow, tired smile and nodded. "Do you remember what you felt before you fell unconscious?"

"I do, but I don't understand it."

"Regret. Feray regrets her decisions and her actions." He was right. I nodded. She was not innocent, but she had realized how much damage her actions had caused. I knew it without any doubt, as I had experienced her feelings as my own. My body shuddered as I remembered the experience.

"How did it happen? How could I feel what Feray was feeling?"

"It wasn't just you. All of us experienced her feelings. Though they affected you much more than us. It was Alia. She is the Mirror. She has a strange ability to reflect a person's feelings. She can feel what her subject is feeling, and she can make others around her experience those feelings as their own. No one knows how it works or why, but it does."

"What did the elders decide about Feray?" I asked.

"Alev had called off the meeting after you fell unconscious. It was proven that Feray was not innocent, but the decision about her fate is still pending. The elders will meet again soon to announce it. But before that, there is another pressing matter."

"What is that?"

Kratos continued, "Looks like there will be another attack. Esmeray wants to steal all the vials of light to keep her beast strong. The council of elders is meeting again. You should rest now. I will let you know what happens."

I did not want to rest. I wanted to attend the meeting. "Can I come with you?"

"If that's what you want," Kratos replied gently.

We left the lodge for the meeting. It was raining again, so it was held at Alev's place. Kratos and I were the first to go to the sitting room for the meeting.

Soon, the elders arrived. Jinyan was the last one to be carried in by two sturdy guardians. Alev waited till everyone was seated and comfortable. Then, she started the meeting.

"Yesterday was a terrible day. We witnessed betrayal, deceit, and cruelty. Our own let us down. But today is a new day. Let's pull ourselves together and prepare for the inevitable battle. The sooner we fight it off, the quicker the peace will be restored."

She paused as everyone listened to her with respect and attention.

"Alia has shown us that Feray was indeed telling the truth. Her actions were misguided and full of pride, but she was tricked by Esmeray to do such a thing."

Jinyan nodded and said, "You are right, Alev! I am sure Feray created the creature as the Seren defender. But it is now in the hands of Esmeray, and she wants to take all the vials. We cannot allow this. We need to stop her."

Boris was next to share his thoughts. "I have read Xahene's journals. I believe he stopped Esmeray using some kind of weapon. He did not survive the fight, or we would have known how to make such a weapon. If we could find out what it was, we would be in a better position to fight back."

Everyone nodded. After a while, Jinyan said, "There is only

one place to find what we don't know about Xahene's weapon."

Alev thought for a while. Then she said decidedly, "We will visit Sere!"

Instantly, the atmosphere in the room changed. Loud gasps were followed by whispering among the Seren elders and guardians. Alev ignored the reaction and continued.

"We will leave early in the morning. Boris! Make preparations for the journey. The weather is bad. We must be back before the evening falls."

Chapter 9

Kratos and I went outside before anyone else. The weather was sad and gloomy, and it was evening already. After Kratos left to rest in the Orangetree chamber, I wandered around the village center for some time. But I was not comfortable out in the open. The rain had left big puddles behind, and there was no place to sit. I was about to head home when Aymelek came and asked for help. I was more than happy to.

We walked toward the glowing Moontree. It looked even more impressive in the dark, and the raindrops hanging on its leaves and flowers gave it a surreal look. Aymelek invited me in, and I looked around. The chamber walls were lined by the usual backless shelves with Moonlight vials. I glanced up at the ceiling and saw a wide opening in the roof. The heavily entwined branches shied away from each other to make the circular opening right in the middle, above the bulb.

Another look at the bulb startled me. The light inside was fading. Aymelek understood the look on my face and said, "It has been raining a lot. On cloudy days, the trees cannot generate enough light to store in the bulb. We used the light to heal Kratos and for the mirror's test. The Moontree needs more light.

It is dangerous for the tree to run out of its light. We need to pour the light from the vials on the shelf onto the bulb, careful not to spill any. We cannot afford to waste any amount."

Cautiously, we brought the vials to the bulb one after the other and poured them onto the top, middle part connected to the branches. The fruit absorbed the light and stored it inside, slowly filling the bulb.

As we did this, Aymelek surprised me with a new revelation. The seven trees around the Whitetree provided their beneficial healing effect when the Moontree had Moonlight in its fruit. If the Moontree ran out, the others stole the light from all living things nearby and refilled the bulb in the mother tree.

Without the Moonlight, the trees would destroy instead of heal. Aymelek didn't know how long the clouds would continue to darken the sky, and then there was an upcoming battle to think of. She was worried that the trees could turn against us if the Moonlight ran out.

She pointed toward the shelves. "These shelves were glowing with Moonlight yesterday. Now, they are empty. Deserted. Feray used most of it for her ambition. Moonlight is difficult to collect, and it is vital for the Seren. Yet, she wasted it so callously. She didn't care for her people. Alev is right. She doesn't deserve our kindness."

I was sad for Aymelek. She deserved loyalty, yet she received indifference and cruelty from her mentor. I didn't try to console her. I understood that nothing could comfort her at the time.

The guardians stayed outside the trees as we walked out toward our homes. On our way, I asked Aymelek about the place we were going to in the morning. Aymelek reminded me of its name, "Sere." Then she added, "It's a cursed place, a ruin. A place that has seen the battle between Xahene and Esmeray and was destroyed by it."

"Why do the elders want to go there?" Sere sounded dangerous and scary.

"It is cursed, but it is where Xahene recorded his memories. If there is any hope of finding any answers, we will find them there," Aymelek explained.

Aymelek left on a different path for her home, and I continued on to my own. The rain started again.

The rain was gentle but loud. The waterfalls ran aggressively, and the nearby forest was full of the sounds of the night. Outside my home, I noticed footprints in the mud. There was someone there. I walked the boardwalk slowly to not create a sound and went over the fence to the backyard. I reached the back window as silently as I could and peeked inside. I saw a figure sitting on the chair, looking toward a lit fireplace inside the house. His back was toward me, and a cloak hid his head. Without turning or looking at me, he said, "Come inside! Let's talk."

My knees weakened, and I gasped in fear. I started to shiver and felt sweat forming on my body, even as the rain washed it away.

The hooded figure spoke again, "Come inside. We need to talk."

I was scared, and an even scarier thought came to my mind. I asked, "Are you the wizard?"

The hooded figure slowly turned its face toward me and moved the head covering back to expose himself. "It's me, Qilam. It is cold outside. Come in. We need to talk."

I knew that the guardians were looking for Qilam. For a moment, I thought of running to the village to tell them that he was in my home, but then I decided against it. He could easily run away and disappear into the forest by the time I come back with the guardians. He had chosen to come to me because I was alone. I decided to hear what he had to say. His past warning had helped the Seren, after all. I walked to the front and entered the home. After drying myself, I sat down next to him, and we looked at each other silently. The fire crackled loudly in the fireplace. I stayed quiet, still nervous, as I waited for him to speak.

"Esmeray..." he said and stopped abruptly.

"What about her?" I inquired.

He thought for a moment and then responded in a monotonous tone, "She has been talking to me. She wanted me to join her. She thought I would be mad at everyone for blaming and ignoring me after Alfred left. She told me her plans to take the vials. I do not want to hurt anyone, so I told her that I would not join her. She threatened me. That is why I have been hiding. I had to inform the village of the impending attack. After that, I ran and hid in the forest."

I nodded. It made sense. Qilam leaned forward and spoke urgently, "I did not want to come to you and put you in any danger, but I have nowhere else to go. Esmeray is looking for me. I had to come here to tell you about her next plan."

The fireplace crackled, then a loud boom of thunder outside shook me. The atmosphere added to my fears. I tried to calm myself and asked, "What does Esmeray intend to do?"

"Firstly, I believe that she could very well be the wizard. It makes her way more dangerous than we anticipated. During my research, I have found many things about the wizard. These things help me understand her mindset. Therefore, I can predict her next move."

He looked right in my eyes and said the horrible words, "She will burn down the Tree Circle if she cannot have all the vials. You need to convince the elders to let her take them. This is the only way to get rid of her. It's a price we have to pay to protect Serenus."

"She is already so dangerous. Why would the elders do that?"

"Because once she has the vials, she plans to leave the island."

"And what if she takes the vials and doesn't leave the island? She will be more powerful than ever, and we will not be able to do anything."

He responded casually, "If she is the wizard, which I believe she is, she doesn't care about Serenus. She wants to go to the next islands and find the lost scroll. She wants ultimate and un-challenged power. Nothing less will satisfy her. To her, the Seren and their lives are meaningless. Her ambitions are everything.

If she can go, she will. But if she can't, she will burn everything and destroy everyone who stands in her way."

The elders were already worried about the same thing. I agreed with Qilam's words and told him about the meeting with the elders. I skipped the part about the visit to Sere the following day but assured him that the elders were planning to fight her and they wouldn't give up the vials.

Anger twisted Qilam's face. "They are so irrational. They cannot fight her. She will destroy the Tree Circle. They should hand over the vials and let her leave forever. It's a small price to pay to save the island." He paused and then reinforced his words with another argument, "It is an opportunity for us to get rid of the wizard forever. I think we should take it."

His argument was sound, but I understood that we couldn't trust that Esmeray would leave after she had all the power.

"The elders won't listen to me, and I have important things to do. You need to persuade the elders."

Qilam's words worried me. I asked, "What are you planning to do?"

Taken aback by the question, he said, "Me? Nothing. I don't plan on doing anything except finding a new hiding place. I am just saying that we should take the offer, but I don't intend to play any role. I have already put my life at risk by warning you about the attack. I have made her my enemy. Yes, I want her to leave forever so that I can live in peace, but it is also in the best interest of everyone in Serenus."

We sat quietly for a while. Then I asked, "Are you hungry?

Would you like something to eat?" He nodded. I brought him fruit and some bread with soup. As he ate, I thought about his words.

"How are you sure she will take the vials and leave?" I repeated my question.

"People like her are power-hungry. The power of the beast is not enough for her. She wants the lost scroll. We have searched this island for generations, and we are quite sure that the scroll is not here. She needs to go to the lands past the dark veil. She wants a position of power in the next world, which is why she needed the beast. Now, she needs the light vials to make the journey. If we let her go, it would help her, but it also helps us. Think about it. Never having to worry about the evil wizard again. Isn't that the best for Serenus?"

"Yes, but what if she doesn't leave?" I asked in exasperation.

"Then we are in big trouble, me more than others," he responded with a shaky voice.

He had risked everything to warn us of the attack on the village. His warning triggered the elders who placed armed guardians around the trees. That was probably why Esmeray had to leave with the beast without taking the vials. He had done everything an honest villager would do. But I knew what others thought about him. They knew him better than I did, and I couldn't ignore their suspicions about him so easily. But I didn't want Qilam to know my thoughts, so I let him feel that I felt obliged to him for his role and expressed my gratitude.

"I am as much a part of this island as anyone else," he said.

"They may think my ideas are crazy or even dangerous, but I can't allow anyone to harm Serenus."

I asked him to stay for the night. He agreed. "I am very grateful. I will not bother you too much and leave early in the morning."

We sat quietly for some more time, listening to the rain and the night sounds, watching the fireplace. I put more wood in the fire and asked him, "What do you know about the lost scroll?"

His eyes shone with excitement as he said, "The lost scroll? It is a very powerful knowledge that was lost in time."

"Most of the Seren seem to think it's just a story. Do you think it's real?" I asked.

"Yes, I do. As real as you and me. More real, even. It is the only thing that is real in this world," Qilam chanted passionately.

"What do you mean by that?"

"I don't think this world is real. It is just a test. Real-life starts after you pass this test. I think the finder of the scroll will move on to live a real life that will be everlasting. Everlasting life for an all-powerful wizard." He spoke prophetically as I looked at his glowing face.

"You see, we are not just this." He pointed at himself and me. "We are so much more than this body."

"You want the lost scroll?" I asked directly.

"Every sensible, smart person should want the lost scroll. Finding it is the goal of this life, and once found, it will wake you to the world beyond all worlds."

The more I listened to him, the less I trusted his words. I wondered what the source of this information was. "How do you know this?"

"Oh, I know. Trust me. I was born with this knowledge. You know how some Seren come to this island with magical abilities? I came with a voice that speaks in my head."

His words were absurd. "And what does this voice tell you? Where do we come from?" I asked mockingly.

"You don't believe me? Didn't you hear the warning in your dream when you first woke up in the boat? Didn't you hear the voice?"

"Yes, everyone hears that. The voice in the dream wants to wake us up." I replied.

"Right." He moved forward on his chair. Now, he was sitting at the edge, leaning toward me, looking straight into my eyes. "I hear it every day. And this voice talks to me about things you cannot imagine."

"Like what?"

"It speaks of a world beyond all the worlds. The one where we are gods. It calls me to itself. It is waiting for me there." He paused, running his hand through his messy beard, "The voice wants me to go after the lost scroll and become an all-powerful wizard. It says it is my mission, everyone's mission."

Qilam was past his middle years and had clearly failed at his job as a thinker. I thought he was going mad, and that's why he heard these voices in his head. But I knew he wouldn't care what I thought of his words.

He continued speaking passionately, "You know, you and I are not different. We are the same. You question the things that other people don't question. Everyone in the village lives this life as if it is the real world. It is not. You and I know that we have come from somewhere and have to go somewhere. We have not reached our destination yet. Our future is wide open and full of amazing journeys. It is such a loss that people waste their lives."

He was not hiding behind his words anymore and spoke clearly, so I asked, "What if you are wrong and there is no next world? What if anyone who left Serenus died without ever reaching another land?"

All his excitement vanished, and he moved back in his chair. He stared at the fireplace and spoke in a monotonous voice, "Then I am the biggest idiot who has ever lived, and the voices in my head are lying to me. But I have no way of knowing for sure. I only know what I know, and there is only one way to know more" His voice became confident once again, and he perked up in the chair. "I will go looking for the next world to find out. Oh, and I have one more reason for you to believe me. I have never told anyone about it. But I want you to know."

I didn't believe him, but at the same time, I wanted to know what he was talking about. "What is it?"

"I woke up with the poem like everyone did, but I also had

another page with me." My eyes opened wide as he searched his pockets and produced a badly crumpled paper. He straightened it and handed it to me, then asked me to read it. I read it out loud:

"Train from the pod, prove your worth,

Grow into a god beyond this earth.

Very few are winners, and big is our need,

Overcome the failures, and then proceed.

There's more to try if a branch will fail,

No reason to cry and nothing to wail,

We'll trace back to one and then reseed,

To find the one who will succeed."

I looked at Qilam in disbelief. He said, "I've never met another person who came with this poem. I have it. It must mean something. I am supposed to play a role. Though, I don't know what."

I was shocked at what he was saying. He had another poem that nobody else had. How could I trust it? What if he wrote it himself? He could be crazy enough to believe in his own made-up stories.

One thing was clear: Qilam believed in it blindly. But there was no way for me to know if any of this was real.

I conveyed my thoughts openly. "I started in a boat and had a poem and a watch. Someone gave it to me for a reason. The watch is also mysterious. No one seems to know what it is about. This much I understand, and I agree that there could be much more than we know, but how you leap from this to the desire to try going into the dark is beyond me. The island is quite large, and there are mysteries in even the smallest things. How do you know that the verse, the world is so vast, refers to other worlds?"

He read the verses from the poem: "'Grow into a god beyond this earth.' 'Catch the wizard, go past the fall.' These are all very clear instructions."

"So, why are you still here?" I was annoyed by his beliefs and efforts to convince others while he was afraid of trying it for himself.

"I guess I lack the courage to find out if I'm right or wrong. You are right in your observation. I should have gone into the dark a long time ago."

"No, I don't mean you should have gone into the dark. I mean, you shouldn't preach to others what you don't fully believe in yourself. And if you really believed in it, you wouldn't be here."

I had made up my mind about him. And I knew that he had convinced Alfred and four others to go into the dark with his words while he was still here sitting in my warm and comfortable home, trying to convince me that it was worth going into the Dark End.

He confused me with his next words. "You are right. I should do what I believe in. I will go to the next world. I just need to do one thing first."

He relaxed considerably as if he had really made up his mind.

"What is it that you need to do?" I asked.

"I want to see Esmeray defeated. Only so I can leave with the peace of mind knowing that Serenus is safe."

We sat in front of the fire for a long time, immersed in our own thoughts. I got up when I was too tired to think clearly and asked Qilam to rest as well.

Chapter 10

I woke up early in the morning when I heard a knock on the door. Before opening it, I looked around for Qilam, but he wasn't there. He must have left already. He had cleaned up after himself, and there was no sign of him ever being here. I opened the door and invited Idir inside.

"We will be leaving for Sere soon," he reminded me as he came inside.

"Yes, I will get ready quickly," I replied.

He helped me in starting a fire to make breakfast. We ate together, and I kept thinking about my conversation with Qilam. I did not want to tell anyone what he said about the other poem or his plans to go into the dark, but I had to reveal the threat of the attack.

I said softly, "Qilam visited me last night."

Idir jumped in surprise. "What did he want?"

"He said Esmeray will destroy the Tree Circle if we don't hand over all the vials of light," I explained her horrible plan.

Idir gasped and stood up abruptly. "We need to leave right

now. The elders should know Esmeray's plan before it's too late."

We left everything as it was and ran out toward the village center. We could no longer wait to finish breakfast. The warning, once again, was dire.

We met Aymelek on her way to the trees and found Kratos in the elder's home. The worry on our faces scared everyone. I told the news of another attack.

"Qilam came to me last night and told me that Esmeray will burn down the Tree Circle and kill everyone who will stand in her way unless we give her the vials of light. He believes that she will leave this world forever and go into the Dark End." I tried to be as concise as possible.

Alev raised her brows. "Esmeray will take everything she ever wanted and then just go into the dark? Why would she do that? That makes no sense."

I tried to explain, "Qilam believes that Esmeray wants to go to the next world with a weapon that could ensure her a place of power there."

Alev interrupted me, "And why is Qilam not coming to us with this information? Why is he hiding?"

"He warned us of the attack on the village. Because of that, Esmeray could not take the vials before the beast came alive. He is afraid she will kill him—that is why he is hiding," I clarified.

Boris spoke this time. "I wonder why Esmeray can't kill him when she goes to tell him her plans?"

"No. It is not what you think. Esmeray wanted Qilam to join

her. She thought he would not care about Seren because they didn't believe him and left him alone. He didn't join her but knew her plans. He shared her plans with us. That is why his life is in danger. We shouldn't doubt his intentions. He already saved the vials from Esmeray." I defended Qilam and tried to show them his perspective. "We should be grateful for what he has done for everyone."

Boris laughed a smug laugh. "And why does a powerful wizard want Qilam to join her? What could she get out of his companionship? Some crazy thoughts and a life void of any useful action? In what way has he ever contributed to Serenus? He is a complete nuisance. No one wants to be with him." He turned to me. "You are too naïve."

Alev addressed us sternly, "Stop arguing, both of you! It is great that Qilam came to...." She looked at me and asked, "Have you picked a name yet?" I shook my head. She was clearly disappointed but continued, "For now, nothing changes. We will continue with our plans. We need to find a way to stop Esmeray. Boris! Do what you can to defend against another attack. And hide two guardians near No Name's house. I want Qilam captured if he shows up again."

I left with my head held low and waited outside as the caravan got ready for the visit to Sere. Idir joined me, and we zigzagged around the huge puddles in the village center.

The rain had put out the fire and smoke but couldn't wash away the memories of the terrible day. The broken, burned houses reminded me of the vicious attack. The Seren were working diligently to revive the village. The destroyed trees had been dragged away. I walked on the freshly-cleaned paths without any fear of sharp broken glass hurting my feet. The damaged houses were being repaired or reconstructed according to their damage. I admired my fellow Seren for not giving in to despair. They kept their hopes alive, which gave them the strength to go through the tragedy.

Finally, it was time to go. Once the elders were comfortable in a four-seat cart, the strong guardians pushed it ahead. Two coaches full of supplies followed them.

On our way out of the village, we passed through the forge. The sunlight squeezed through the dark clouds in a feeble attempt to brighten the landscape, but the forge was sad, grey, and silent.

Idir, Aymelek, Boris, and I walked along with the elder's cart. Some guardians led the party while others stayed at the rear. They were dressed in the same delicate-looking armor as those who had arrested me the day I came to Serenus. I wondered how such armor could protect anyone.

Idir smiled as I asked him the question.

"This armor only looks delicate. The forgers are quite skilled at making it light enough to carry but as strong as any. The only problem is that it is useless in protecting them from magical adversaries."

The guardians pushed the cart toward the buildings at the back of the forge. Boris and Idir used scythes to make their way through the overgrown grass between the two buildings. Soon, a path began to take shape, and the cart moved on.

The scent of the freshly cut grass fell soothingly on my fidgety nerves. I felt light and fresh. The thought of our dreary destination slipped out of my mind. We kept walking in sync with the rolling spokes in the wheel of the elder's cart.

Idir and Boris were hard at work. A path was buried under the wild vegetation that had not been walked on in a long time. Idir confirmed my observation. The Seren had abandoned it, and no one walked over it anymore. Nature had reclaimed it and had breathed life back into the ground.

It was a slow and tedious walk through the forest, and we were relieved as we approached a clearing. The forest had grown thin, announcing the end of the forested land. A furious river ran noisily right next to the clearing.

Beyond the river was a strange terrain, black and bleak. Its presence took away the relief of getting near the journey's end. With every step, the Seren grew tense. I sensed it in their silence and their nervous eyes fixed on the grey horizon.

An old, worn-out bridge appeared ahead. The guardians brought the cart to a slow stop near it. Boris went to check the bridge, which creaked loudly under his feet. He walked over its length and declared it safe for the cart.

Across the bridge, a wasteland spread between the river and the horizon at the other end. Tall, towering clouds hung over it, confident of their supremacy over the land. We had reached Sere.

The whole place had burned down sometime in the distant past. The charred tree trunks stood like dark pillars guarding a secret in the depths of the charcoal forest.

We advanced slowly, leaving footmarks on the damp, ashy soil. The lifeless stumps were still mourning for whatever tragedy befell the once-alive forest.

I looked around, searching for a tiny seedling, a blade of grass, or a mushroom, perhaps. The place was devoid of life.

I was surprised at the dark grey, empty vastness. It was unnatural. I would expect a burned forest to be overcrowded with grasses gushing out of the ground and the seedlings sprouting through the fire-fertilized land. I would expect it to be rich and green. Aymelek was the one to sense the cause of its eternal destruction. She was sure it was a work of some evil magic. Was it a spell cast by Esmeray? Everyone believed so, though they couldn't prove it.

The cart moved unsteadily over the uneven, pathless land. We had to go slower. Time passed silently between us.

A large tree grew out of the horizon slowly. It grew larger and larger as we went closer. Alev pointed toward it, saying it was our destination.

We looked at the massive tree in amazement. It was still standing, but most of its bark was gone, burnt away. Only a few thicker branches still remained on it.

Under the tree was a heap of thin, wrinkled, black branches that looked like all life was sucked out of them. What power could have destroyed such an enormous thing? I felt small and vulnerable in the dark, black world.

Alev described the entrance to the tree, and Boris searched for it with another guardian. It took some time to move the branches out of the way, but they found the opening eventually. It was a hollow in the tree trunk, large enough for one person to go through at a time.

Alev insisted on leaving some guardians outside with the cart while asking others to go through the hollow.

The Seren lit the torches and went inside the dark tree trunk. I followed Aymelek and walked into an open space inside it. Alev and Jinyan sat down on dusty wooden chairs inside.

The chairs were already there, along with a large table. Someone had left them there a long time ago. Judging by their size, they had been made right there in the hollow. It was impossible to bring them in through the narrow entrance.

Boris brought some scrolls in and spread them on the table. Others erected the torches in the brackets fixed in the tree walls.

Someone had stayed there and had made the room comfortable. There were dusty scrolls and books in shelves on the tree walls.

"Xahene was a thinker," Alev said, "and this is where he used to come to be alone with his thoughts for days at a time. He recorded many of his thoughts here before he was lost. Search the place and see what we can learn from here." Alev pointed to the walls. "These walls are the keepers of Xahene's memory and the history of Serenus. Read aloud whatever you can see and note everything. Nothing should be ignored."

The Seren got busy. Everyone went toward the book shelves

while the elders stayed in their chairs. I tried to study the signs and symbols that were drawn on the walls, probably with a sharp tool.

As the words were read, the fragments of an untold past began to emerge. Most of the shelves were covered quickly. Boris was looking at illustrations and drawings in a notebook. I stood by him as he studied them carefully.

Everyone was busy with their work, analyzing and recording the information. We found that some of the writings were unrelated to the incident we were probing. Xahene probably used this place to think about other things too.

Boris saw a note and read it aloud. "A line in the line of thought. It thinks what I think." This note was encircled by a deeply etched line. He repeated it over and over again. It didn't fit anywhere in the story. No one came up with an answer to justify the important-looking line. After thinking about it for some time, Jinyan figured it might be essential and ordered Boris to note it down for later consideration.

Idir stood by, holding a notebook in his hand with a bitter look on his face. I moved closer and asked if everything was okay. He handed me the notebook. I began to read it. I was only a couple of pages in, and I was shocked by the words I was reading. It was Xahene's journal. Alev had introduced Xahene as a thinker, and we were here looking for help from his records, but from what I was reading, it was clear that Xahene did not think so highly of himself. His words portrayed a very stark picture. He wrote of his failures and struggles in life. He thought he was a disappointment at everything he tried as if there was a darkness inside of him keeping him from greatness. I had imagined a heroic figure who defeated Esmeray and saved Serenus, but it turned out that he was full of self-doubt and consumed by his perceived failures and negativity.

Idir saw the sad look on my face and explained, "It is true. Xahene lived a difficult life. People called him lazy and useless, and he thought it to be true. He felt incompetent, unsure of himself, and had trouble keeping up with life. He was a depressed Seren."

I sat down with the journal and started reading more. Xahene had written accounts of how people around him did not understand him. He was frustrated by it and felt alone at the mercy of depression. On many pages, I noticed that he would start writing a thought but then leave it unfinished as if it wasn't important enough, or maybe he didn't have the energy to finish it. The journal was full of incomplete ideas and stories. On one of the pages, he wrote a dream he had while sitting under the Yellowtree. It was a horrible dream. He saw himself lying on the ground, covered in filth. All the troubles of his life were keeping him down. His problems appeared in the form of a monster that kept a foot on his neck. He was unable to get up and get rid of it. It was just too sad. I couldn't read anymore and returned the journal to Idir.

Idir tried to console me, "Don't worry. He was eventually able to get rid of it. He lived to his full potential. Imagine if he could know then that his actions would save the world from a powerful wizard one day. He spent all that time in misery - thinking less of himself; such a waste."

Boris found something and called everyone to look at it. We left Xahene's journal and went to see what he had discovered.

It was an illustration with six circles that sat on an arc, with straight lines shooting from every circle and joining at a single point ahead. Their meeting point was the center of a smaller circle that gave out a thick, wavy line. That was all we could understand from this illustration.

Aymelek thought it looked familiar. She couldn't say for sure, but she remembered seeing something similar in the scrolls at the healer's house.

Alev, too, was interested in the circles. "They do look familiar. Six circles on an arc and one in the middle collecting something from the others and sending it out."

Nothing came out of it. Alev asked everyone to recheck the walls for anything they might have missed. The Seren moved around the room again and confirmed that everything related to the incident had been recorded in Boris's scrolls.

"Time to leave, then. Let's get back before it gets dark," Jinyan said urgently.

Alev asked the guardians to put everything that contained Xahene's writing in the cart with supplies. Gathering the scrolls and notebooks didn't take long. Soon, we were out of the tree room and on our way back.

The last rays of the sun were brighter before the evening came. We must have missed a strong wind while in the tree room. The towering clouds had dispersed, letting the sun warm the damp land before the colder evening arrived.

We reached back at the village as the day gave way to dusk. Everyone needed a thorough wash. The Sere had left its dark marks on our hands, feet, and clothes alike. I rubbed my hands on my clothes to clean them. But the black was stubborn.

As we reached the village center, our companions went their separate ways. Alev announced a meeting in the morning, and the elders left. Boris, Aymelek, Idir, and I went to the healer's home. We passed through the deserted village center. It would take some more days for the Seren to finally eat their midday meals together.

A warm bowl of soup welcomed me with an appetizing, tangy aroma. I felt great once the long, warm bath washed away the charcoal. Idir and Boris had joined me after they came back from their homes, all fresh and clean. I enjoyed my meal thoroughly.

The front door opened smoothly. It was Kratos. He had not joined us in the journey to Sere as, considering his health, Alev had strictly forbidden it. He had stayed in the Orangetree all day and had come to ask about our trip.

"Hey!" I shouted excitedly upon seeing Kratos walking in the kitchen with slow but steady steps.

He asked me if I was alright. I nodded happily.

Kratos had made a special place in my heart. Seeing him healthy and safe was a great feeling.

He demanded we tell him whatever he had missed. Idir recounted everything that had happened in Sere. Boris and Aymelek joined him. I sat quietly and listened.

Then Boris asked, "Kratos! you never told us how you confronted Esmeray and got hurt."

Kratos replied, "I had gone to Feray to talk about the old lady and the conversation this one heard that night." He pointed to me and asked, "Pick a name yet?"

I shook my head, and everyone laughed. Kratos smiled and resumed his tale.

"I met Feray at the front door and told her that I wanted to talk to her. She wanted us to sit outside, but I insisted we go into the house. She was quite hesitant, just like you said she was with you. I didn't listen to her excuses and entered the house despite her protests. The old lady was there by the front door, eavesdropping on us. Feray panicked when I asked who she was. She had no answer. I decided to confront the old lady myself. I demanded to know who she was and how she had come to Serenus. She didn't answer. Instead, she muttered something under her breath, and I felt I had been hit in the chest. That's all I remember."

Boris had noted down his statement along with the other incidents recorded previously. It disturbed everyone.

Idir changed the subject. "So, what now?"

Aymelek looked at the illustrations in Boris's scrolls. "We must look this illustration up in the healer's scrolls. Tidy up the table. I will bring the scrolls here."

I got up to help her with the scrolls. The healer's library was small, with cupboards lining three walls from the ceiling to the floor. Aymelek picked dusty scrolls from one shelf. We carried them to the kitchen table in our arms.

The torches flickered on the symbols on the scrolls. I looked at them absentmindedly. Others were going through them one by one, trying to find anything that could explain Xahene's illustration.

"Why don't you go and get some rest, Kratos?" Aymelek suggested. "You need sleep. We will come get you as soon as we find something."

Kratos argued that he had rested a lot already. It was time to work. But Aymelek ignored his grumbling and made him leave. I followed him out of the healer's home and inside the Orangetree. I returned once he was comfortable in bed.

The search through the scrolls went all night. At some point, I fell asleep on the bench.

Bright sunlight came through the window and woke me up. I stretched and sat up.

Kratos was sitting quietly nearby. He looked healthy. He asked, "Did you sleep well?"

"Yeah. I slept like a log. Just woke up."

He watched me with concern. "How have you been? It must be difficult for you to witness such troubles."

"Honestly, it was quite scary. But most of all, I was scared for you. Aymelek and Idir have been very good to me."

"You are strong. Idir told me how you took care of me. I am really grateful for what you did."

Idir called us loudly from the sitting room. His voice carried excitement. We went out quickly, eager to learn the reason for his enthusiasm. "Aymelek has an idea. We believe it will work."

We went to the kitchen buzzing with excited voices. I looked out of the window. The guardians outside reminded me of the unfortunate incident we had all suffered. I saw two Seren leaving the Redtree accompanied by their friends or loved ones. They had recovered and were going back to their homes. Life was getting back to normal.

I ate breakfast as Aymelek showed us the illustrations from the healer's library and Xahene's tree wall. They were precisely the same. The only difference was that the image from the healer's library had symbols written next to the circles sitting on the arc and the one ahead. Idir and Boris had stayed up the whole night to help Aymelek with the search. When they finally found the right scroll, the ordeal of understanding it had taken up the remaining night. They had called the elders to discuss their findings. We waited for them to arrive.

Idir, Kratos, and Boris discussed making the equipment in the drawing while Aymelek checked the scrolls continuously.

The elders came to hear the news, and Aymelek started sharing the conclusion. "This illustration was found in the scrolls from the time of Savita. We believe that Savita and Xahene must have designed it when they thought of ways to deal with Esmeray. Its presence in the library and on Xahene's tree walls is important. I think Xahene recorded it because it worked."

"What exactly is it?" Jinyan voiced his curiosity.

"It looks like a weapon. The illustration from the library has some letters written next to the six circles. It took a painfully long time to understand. But we believe the circles are, in fact, vials containing light from the light trees."

She spread the scroll on a small table Idir had placed in the middle of the room. Everyone leaned forward to see.

Aymelek explained as she pointed to the illustration, "The six circles here on the arc are the vials of red, orange, yellow, green, blue, and indigo, while this circle in the middle is violet. The arrows show that the light from the six circles is focused on the violet vial. As it passes through it, a single beam of light is released."

Alev nodded in agreement. Her face glowed with excitement.

"We know that every light has its distinct power. This weapon joins the powers, and I believe this new light must be more powerful than any magic."

I asked quickly, "What is the violet light for? I didn't see any bulbs or shelves on the violet tree. Isn't it just an entrance arch?"

Aymelek answered, "The violet light is too scarce, so the tree doesn't grow enough to produce a fruit, but we can still collect the light reflected from its flowers and use it."

"What is it used for?"

"It is hard to explain, but basically, it brings balance and order to things," Aymelek said.

Alev listened to her attentively and then asked. "Aymelek!

Do you think this new light would have defeated Esmeray?"

Aymelek replied, "I do. And if we remake this weapon, we might be able to defeat her once again."

"What do you know about this new light?" Jinyan questioned her.

"Well, I don't know. I have been thinking about it. There are two possibilities. It could have all the properties of every source light, or it could have a completely different power of its own."

Jinyan was reluctant to experiment with lights until the effect of the new light was known.

Alev asked Aymelek for the illustration and studied it for some time, then she looked up from the sheet and said, "Savita was fascinated by the lights and their effects on us. Before Esmeray came, she had started experimenting with them. I had worked with her in her experiments. We mixed lights together and made new shades and hues. But we always added the Moonlight to keep the effects positive. Without Moonlight, the lights became aggressive."

Aymelek continued, "I think since this device doesn't take any Moonlight, it must be a weapon that can be used to attack instead of healing someone."

Jinyan was still not convinced. "What about the new light? What if it is not safe? Which light do you think will be produced if we mix the existing ones?"

They began to discuss different possibilities about the new light. I listened to their discussion while studying the illustration. Red, orange, yellow, green, blue, and indigo. All colors of the Light-trees. All, except white. What could it be that has all the colors? I kept repeating the question in my head. And then I rephrased the question. "What could it be that is all colors?"

The realization came suddenly, and without thinking twice, I said it aloud, "Black! It will be black."

Jinyan huffed in annoyance. "Black is darkness. It is the absence of light. There can't be a black light."

I rephrased my words to better convey my thought, "I don't know if I am right or not. I am sure you know that black is not a color in itself. It is all the colors. Perhaps Savita used all the color lights and created something black."

Alev nodded slowly. "I think No Name might be right. We have worked with the lights for so long, and we still don't fully understand what they are capable of." Then she addressed Aymelek, "I would say we try it and see what happens. We will carry out the experiment away from the village. I will accompany you. Everyone else must stay back."

Jinyan agreed reluctantly as others gave their approval. They wanted to test it quickly, so Aymelek left to collect the vials for the experiment. It was decided that everyone else would wait in the healer's house.

Waiting was agonizing. We were excited about the experiment but, at the same time, anxious about the result. It might not turn out as we thought.

We stayed in and took turns to pace in the room. When I couldn't take it anymore, I left the house and went for a stroll in the yard. The weather was pleasant, with sunshine and a clear blue sky extending from horizon to horizon. The floral trees swayed gently in the occasional light breeze.

The yard was mostly empty. The guardians had made sure that no one could go near Alev and Aymelek as they experimented with the lights in the forest.

We ate our midday meal at the healer's house. There was still no news of Alev and Aymelek.

As the time passed, the excitement and thrill turned into worry. We whispered amongst ourselves nervously. Kratos wanted to go and check on them. But Jinyan forbade him from leaving the room. He was even more strict than Alev.

The front door opened, and we rushed toward the sitting room. Aymelek was back, and two guardians were bringing Alev in. They smiled at us broadly.

"We did it," Aymelek said with excitement. "We created the black light."

Aymelek explained how they had to experiment with distances between the vials, and eventually, it worked.

She continued, "The moment I arranged them one last time, the lights sent their rays out in thin, straight lines. They fell on the violet vial without entering it. A beam of glittering black light came out of the vial. I don't know if I should call it light— it looked more like a silk fabric, but intangible. It fell on a plant we chose as our target and completely engulfed it. Then the plant started to wither as the ribbons sucked the life out of it. We had to stop to save the plant, but now we know that it drains life from its target. Both Alev and I studied it carefully. We have no doubt about it being powerful."

Alev agreed. "I am confident about using it against Esmeray. It is pure and mysterious. It exudes a sensation of great power. All we need now is the equipment to carry the source lights in. Aymelek has recorded the amounts of lights and the distances carefully. We already have the illustration to follow. Let's get to it."

Jinyan was happy now that it had been tested. The elders left satisfied. Aymelek explained the recordings she had noted for making the equipment. She wanted a way to keep the violet light vial aside till it was needed. A movable trigger, perhaps. It should align it with others when the equipment is ready to be used.

"It is easy," Kratos assured her. "We won't take long to make the equipment. Just keep the vials ready. Let's give Esmeray a hard time."

Aymelek had terrible news to tell. "The violet light is in an awfully small amount in the Indigotree chamber. We don't have a lot to use."

Kratos provided some much-needed hope, saying, "We will do with what we have. Let's hope it will be enough."

Kratos sat back in the chair and discussed how to make the equipment. Idir moved closer to him, and they were lost in their discussion about finalizing its design.

Boris insisted they call it a weapon. He said it gave him a good feel.

"Alright, Boris! Weapons they are." Idir laughed happily.

Chapter 11

The following two days passed slowly. I stayed in the healer's home most of the time. I was worried Qilam might come to see me if I was in my home. I didn't want him to be captured. I believed he had done the right thing, but the elders still doubted his intentions. Idir often visited me. He explained the different techniques the metal forgers used to make weapons.

The best time of the day was mealtime. I ate my meals with Idir and Boris in the healer's kitchen. They talked about their progress on the weapons. They had made a prototype that Kratos passed after many measurements and questioning. Now, they were replicating it and making more.

We needed nine weapons in total. Aymelek had calculated and informed that only that much Violetlight would be available.

I left the healer's home for a walk. A light breeze lifted my spirits; it felt good to be outside. I went to the village center, which was clean and organized. I was surprised to see how quickly the Seren had completed the repair and reconstruction work. It was like nothing had happened to it except that it still looked empty and deserted. They still had to make benches and tables for the midday meal and gatherings.

As I walked around the village center, some Seren started to gather around me to greet me warmly. They wanted me to tell them how I had saved Kratos. They listened intently and asked questions while I recounted the unfortunate incident. They begged to know more details. I repeated the story with as many details as I could. Eventually, they were satisfied and began to leave. The people were kind, courteous, and polite. I loved being with them. They brought a feeling of belongingness.

Then, I left toward the forge to see how the weapons were being made. Fabio and Misa met me on the way as they were heading to the village center to get food for the workers at the forge. Instead of going to the forge, I walked back with them.

We had a lot to share as we did not meet since the fire. They had been busy with the repairs in the village. We chatted pleasantly as we walked through the village. Suddenly, Fabio stopped and said in a singsong voice, "Here comes Donny!" He shared a meaningful smile with Misa.

I looked at the thin man walking toward us. His eyes moved around constantly, touching everything for just a moment before moving on to the next. He rushed toward me the moment he saw me, almost gliding above the ground, his wings flapping in excitement.

He approached us and asked me with an exaggerated surprise, "Are you…?" Then he came closer and asked Misa, "Is he…?"

His excitement didn't let him complete his sentence.

Misa hid a smile and patted him on the shoulder. "Yes, Donny. He is the one who saved Kratos."

Fabio put his arm around Donny's shoulder and introduced him. "This is Donny, the most intelligent Seren you will ever find."

He looked intelligent with sparkling eyes. Fabio asked, his voice full of respect, "What are you going to enlighten us about today, Donny?"

Donny straightened his shoulders and rubbed his hands together. His gaze fell on me. "Let me tell you how you got here!"

Misa interrupted, "O, enlightened one! He came here like everyone else. In a boat."

Fabio tied his hands behind his back and stood with a bowed head. Something was going on here, but I couldn't understand it. Fabio and Misa were definitely up to something.

Donny looked at them indignantly. "True, but it is never that simple. A lot goes between leaving and arriving." He turned to me, smiling brightly. "I will tell you how you came here." He paused to think for some time, rubbing his chin. "Aha! I've got it!" he announced excitedly. "Move back! Make some space. I need to draw it on the ground for you to understand. You see, such things are not easy to grasp."

Fabio and Misa smiled while we moved back and stood in a semi-circle. Donny picked up a stick and started to draw something on the ground.

First, he drew a circle with the stick, leaving a tiny break where the ends should have joined together.

"This is us, Serenus. Now, you would ask where exactly Serenus is."

He extended the open ends of the circle in straight lines in opposite directions. He walked quite a bit in both directions to draw a long line. It looked like it was touching a circle near the middle. Next, he divided the straight line into many parts by marking short lines.

He continued, "These parts here are the lands. In the beginning, Serenus was on the line, just like all the other lands. Later on, the circumstances demanded that our land drift away. We couldn't leave the line, of course. So…"

Misa and I were as puzzled as Fabio, but he couldn't stop himself and interrupted Donny's narration with, "What exactly is the line?"

Donny replied earnestly. "It is The Line, of course. Where the lands exist."

Clearly, he believed in what he was saying, though it didn't make sense. I listened quietly in the hope of understanding his complex idea.

Donny picked up again. "So, what did we do? We made the land so heavy that the line itself started to curve inwards under its weight till it encircled it completely. See this place?"

Donny pointed to the opening in the circle. "This is where the opening to this world exists." We looked at each other with an amused surprise.

I smiled at Fabio as I slowly understood the reason behind their secretive smiles. Fabio nodded to affirm my observation, but we stayed quiet and listened.

"You cannot just walk through this opening. Till you go around the circle." Donny got up and clapped his hands to dust off the invisible dirt. "After you went around, you walked the length of the circle around the line. No one can imagine the hardships you faced, the places you saw. You proved your worth by staying steadfast. And finally, your labor paid off. You were deemed worthy of getting in the most magnificent land of all, Serenus."

Fabio and Misa burst into laughter as Donny completed his absurd tale. He ignored their laughter and asked me, "That's how it was, right?"

His eyes twinkled. He waited in hopeful anticipation for my response.

I hesitated. He had narrated the story with such excitement and conviction that it was difficult for me to discourage him. I fidgeted with my hands. Donny was now hovering a foot or so above the ground, his wings flapping in excitement. Fabio and Misa were still laughing uncontrollably.

Reluctantly, I replied, "I am sorry, but no. This is not how I came here."

His eyes lost a bit of luster, and he craved affirmation. "But it was close, right?"

I felt terrible for the poor fellow who wanted so badly to be correct. I hated to answer, but what else could I say? "Not even close."

His wings slowly brought him back to the ground. He thought for a moment, then shrugged off the disappointment. "I can think it over again. I'll be right next time."

Fabio had gotten over the laughing fit by now. He patted Donny's shoulder. "Enough for today. Think about it and tell us another time."

Donny walked away, muttering under his breath.

"That was fun," Misa said with a laugh.

Fabio laughed back. "Someone has been sitting under the Yellowtree for far too long."

We picked up food from the village kitchen, and Fabio and Misa talked about Donny's absurd stories on our way back to the forge.

The clanking of metal welcomed us as we reached the path to the forge. I strolled leisurely, looking around at nothing in particular. Fabio and Misa left me to start their work.

The forge had been repaired. There was no sign of the terrible metal structures I had seen the last time I was there.

Idir waved for me. "Hey, come quick. See what we have made?" He took me to the hearth. I greeted other forgers helping Idir.

"The Blacklight bows are ready. Boris named them." Idir

showed me how they worked and asked me to try one. I was quite hesitant as I had never even touched a weapon before. On Idir's insistence, I picked one and tried it. It was straightforward to use.

The Violetlight vial sat off-center. Pushing a small lever moved it in place. We checked every one of them, pushing the lever many times. They worked perfectly.

"Great, the bows are ready. Let's carry these to the healer's yard. Aymelek would be happy to see them." Idir and I carried them. They were lighter than they looked.

We walked back to the healer's yard and carefully stacked the bows on the table in the sitting room. Aymelek was in the kitchen preparing a meal. I helped her chop vegetables and wash fruit. She looked anxious.

"What's the matter?" I asked.

"It will be a full moon in two days. Esmeray will be at her strongest. I fear that is when she will attack. Today, it is cloudy. If we could fight her tonight, we'd have a better chance at winning."

"But we can't fight her till she attacks. She has to come to us," I reminded her.

Aymelek responded quickly, "There might be another way. As a healer, I can call the light. The beast is alive by the power of Moonlight. I can sense it on the island, and I believe I can call it to come to us."

Shocked, I said, "What? You can call the beast? Are you sure it will listen to your call?"

"The Moonlight. I can call the Moonlight, and the beast will be forced to come, and with it, I think Esmeray will come to protect her weapon."

Idir and Boris left their chairs and dashed toward Aymelek as they heard her plan.

"You can call it?" Boris asked with wide eyes.

"Every healer can call the lights. That is how we capture them."

Soon, they were convinced that it was better to surprise Esmeray with an attack instead of waiting for her to pick a time that suited her.

Boris left to discuss it with the elders as Idir brought Kratos and told him about Aymelek's plan. In no time, the elders came and asked about the weapons. Kratos assured them that they were as ready as possible with the available vials of light.

It was decided that Aymelek would call the beast tonight.

Aymelek's idea of calling the Moonlight thrilled me. But at the same time, I was scared too. Everything might not go according to plan. No one knew how strong Esmeray was. If Blacklight bows couldn't take her down, what would happen?

"We need to evacuate the villagers into the forest," Boris said hurriedly. Alev nodded, and he left to make the necessary arrangements.

I walked out with Boris, who was now talking to his guardians. They were making a plan to evacuate the Seren villagers. They would be sent to the deep forest before dark.

"We need a group of armed guardians hiding around the yard. We have nine Blacklight bows. I need the bow bearers to be hiding closer to the yard," Boris continued.

Aymelek wanted to call the beast to the healer's yard. She believed that the Blacklight bows would work better if they stayed closer to the Lighttrees.

"Kratos, Idir, and I will take one bow each," Boris said. He looked at me and inquired, "What about you? Will you go with the villagers?"

"I don't want to go anywhere. I will stay here."

As scary as the idea of being close to the action was, it was exciting and full of adventure. I wanted to be there to witness whatever happened.

No one slept throughout the night. The village was awake and busy. The guardians gathered the villagers in the village center. They had been asked to bring some provisions along if they had to stay away for longer. When the guardians were satisfied that everyone was there, the evacuation started in small groups.

Every group was accompanied by two guardians. The elders were the last to leave. Alev had decided to stay with Aymelek and was taken to the healer's house.

Everyone was on edge now. Aymelek wanted to practice calling the Moonlight. It was overcast, but we could still see the moon between the cracks in the clouds. It wasn't a full moon, so she couldn't collect a lot of light, but she could practice her skills and be ready for the fight.

I followed her out of the healer's home. Once we were alone near the Moontree, she revealed why she wanted to practice. Feray had never allowed her to capture Moonlight. She had requested Alev to be there in case she needed any help. I was worried, but she was convinced that it was the same process. She just wanted to practice once before she tried it in the fight.

I was too anxious now. What if Aymelek couldn't call the Moonlight? Esmeray could attack at a full moon, and we would lose our chance to defeat her. I accompanied Aymelek inside the Whitetree. Alev was already there waiting for us. Together, we waited for the moon to appear from behind the clouds.

The white sphere shone brightly in the sky. It illuminated the land underneath graciously. Aymelek sat in front of the bulb, holding an empty vial. Her eyes were closed. The Moonlight in the vials on the wooden shelves glowed brighter than usual in the dark. Their white glow filled the moon chamber with a sense of peace.

Aymelek looked like an angel with shimmering wings fluttering occasionally. It was difficult to understand if the Moonlight bestowed her the glow or if she emanated the Whitelight that bathed everything in the chamber.

I stood, mesmerized, next to Alev. Her eyes were fixed on the opening in the woody ceiling. It was time.

The Moonlight entered the chamber and fell on the ground

near the white bulb. Aymelek waited as it slowly crept toward her. Any moment now. The Moonlight drew closer. We held our breath. Even time stopped breathing lest it disturbed the miracle.

Pale white rays broke out of their sphere and ran toward the White bulb. Blinding Whitelight spread in every direction like a persistent lightning bolt. The air vibrated with energy. I experienced peace like never before. My mind was silent. I felt every part of my being in vivid detail. My heart beat rhythmically, filling me with life and energy. Pure air entered my lungs and spread through my body, lingering there to cleanse it. It left when it was satisfied, taking away every impurity it could find.

The peaceful light started to diminish slowly. I became aware of my surroundings as the light from the moon caressed the bulb one last time before moving away. Aymelek was still there, holding the glass vial. It was not empty anymore. At the very bottom was a small, white glowing string.

The moon sailed over the sky, and the chamber regained its usual ambiance. My mind woke up, welcoming the rush of thoughts as I lost the awareness I had experienced before. I realized I had missed the chance to see Aymelek catching the Moonlight. I was too busy feeling my own being. Well, I could ask her later how she did it. I was content with the experience.

Aymelek put the Moonlight vial on a nearby shelf and turned toward us with a slow, satisfied smile. We smiled back at her. She had done it—she had captured her first Moonlight. Alev instructed her to fill up the vials for the Blacklight bows. We went to each tree, one after another. Aymelek took empty vials from the shelves and filled them up. It was incredible. She would put her hand in the large vials and bring the light strings out, and then pour them into the small vials. One after the other, they were filled until they were ready to use in the bows.

It took the guardians some time to take the light vials to the healer's house from every Lighttree. They were very delicate and fragile, so they had to be carried carefully.

Boris informed Alev that the guardians had moved all remaining vials from tree chambers to a secret location. Elders had decided to take this step as a precaution. Just in case we couldn't stop Esmeray.

Aymelek and Idir fixed the vials in their proper places and put the ready bows aside.

Kratos entered with the guardians, carrying the Redlight vials. He looked fresh and active. He studied the Blacklight bows cautiously and announced that they were perfect.

It was almost midnight when all the bows were loaded and ready. I asked Aymelek, "Are you sure you will be able to call the beast? You will need to keep it from fleeing when it is attacked by the bows."

Aymelek whispered her response, "You saw how the Moonlight spread around the room when the white bulb reflected it. If you or Alev had a vial with you, it would have stayed empty. I called the Moonlight with my mind, coaxed it gently, and it listened to me. It felt comfortable with me and agreed to stay with me. Though the beast is far away yet, I am sure I can force it to come by coaxing the Moonlight it carries. And once it comes close, it will be much easier to keep it here."

Kratos, Idir, and Boris took their bows. Boris had brought armor for Kratos and Idir as well. The forgers looked like proper warriors now. We decided to divide the bow bearers into groups of four and five. Kratos, Idir, Boris, and two others were the first group. I didn't know anyone from the other group. The second group would take over when and if the first one ran out of lights. They went to hide in the forest, staying close as Aymelek feared the bows might not work effectively if they were far from their target.

Boris had allocated a hiding spot to me. It was in the trees near the healer's house. I was away from the fight and still had a good view.

My heart was beating faster as time passed. I kept my eyes fixed on Aymelek. She sat on the ground near the Moontree with her eyes closed. The battle had started. She was calling the beast. I was close enough to see her face tense as she struggled to contact the Moonlight vibrating in the beast's body. My heart was beating fast. I tried to calm myself and took long breaths.

Aymelek's face relaxed. Maybe she was in contact with the Moonlight. Time slowed down. Nothing moved. I waited. My mind had a mind of its own. It brought terrible thoughts to scare me. What if the Blacklight bows didn't work? Blacklight! There wasn't even such a thing. Even the name sounded silly. I started to sweat. We were idiots. All of us. Me, Kratos, Aymelek, everyone. How could we possibly think we could fight a wizard with as silly a thing as the Blacklight bows? I lost all hope. Esmeray was coming with the terrible creature. And the Seren had glass vials of light for weapons. The sweat drops slithered down my forehead. My hands were moist with anxiety.

Aymelek's alarmed voice brought me out of my thoughts: "It is coming."

I heard Boris next, "Aymelek! Is she close? Can you feel the beast now?"

"I can't judge the distance exactly, but it is close!" she yelled back.

Idir joined the conversation. "How long do we have to wait? Just give us a guess."

Aymelek closed her eyes, and everyone became silent.

A low, muffled sound broke the silence. It grew louder and louder. Something was moving toward us. Fear rushed through me. Aymelek was right. The beast was coming. Would the Blacklight bows work? They had not even been tested on one with magic.

Chapter 12

The sound came closer. It changed from the slow, muffled noise to a loud swishing grunt piercing through the air.

The gigantic beast appeared on the horizon, flapping its metallic wings and swishing its snake-like tail furiously. It shined gold and silver in the dim light.

Aymelek opened her eyes and fixed them on the beast. It appeared to be looking back at her, spreading its dark shadow across the yard. Its wings thundered to threaten Aymelek. She looked so small and insignificant, yet she stayed calm. There was not a hint of fear on her face. Her courage amazed me. With a loud crash, the beast landed in front of her. Someone was sitting on its staunch neck. I peered through the bush I was hiding behind. It was Esmeray. She addressed Aymelek in a loud voice.

"Where is Feray? Is she trying to control my dragon? Feray! Come out. Talk to me." Her voice was proud.

Aymelek responded calmly, "Feray is not here. I am the Seren healer now. I called the beast."

"A new healer?" Esmeray laughed mockingly. "What do you

think you are doing? Do you believe you can fight me? I am Esmeray. I am the most powerful wizard in this world. You dare to call me? You will pay for your insolence with your life and the life of every Seren. I will give you one last chance—surrender the Light vials, and no one has to die. I will leave this world forever. Deny me, and I will take the vials by force and destroy the trees you depend on."

Aymelek spoke in an angry voice, "We have defeated you before, and we will defeat you again. Nobody believes in a word you say. Surrender the beast. You can go in the dark, but not with the light."

Esmeray laughed an evil laugh. "I was hoping you would say that. Now that you have called me, I will let you witness the destruction of your land first-hand. After that, I will take the vials and destroy the Moontree. Your stubbornness will cost you everything."

She held a hand up and started muttering. Her hand caught fire. In a moment, it grew into a giant fireball.

Esmeray looked terrifying, sitting on her beastly creature with a fire burning in her hand. Fear blanketed my senses. I screamed loudly as Esmeray turned her hand toward the ground and released the fireball.

Black silk shot out from every corner of the yard. It rushed toward Esmeray and engulfed her. The fireball fizzed past Aymelek and fell on the grassy ground. The green grass caught fire instantly.

Esmeray shrieked violently as the black silk tried to wrap

itself around her. She lost power over her beast, and it slumped down motionless. She fell to the ground.

Esmeray cast another spell. The black silk started to recede. She stood up slowly, giving force to the spell with continuous muttering under her breath. She was powerful. I feared that the Blacklight bows would not be able to compete with her power.

The second group of Blacklight warriors came out of the forest, hovering in the air, and shot their weapons at Esmeray. Their faces were strained by the effort of holding the bows in position. It seemed as if she were pushing them away.

Esmeray held her hands high with glassy eyes staring emptily in the air. The Blacklight kept struggling against the barrier her spell had created. It was like a protective bubble around her. Her hands caught fire again. It grew bigger and bigger. At the same time, the Blacklight shrank back. The bows must have been running out of light. The warriors threw their bows and ran toward the forest as Esmeray threw balls of fire at them, lighting up everything in their path.

The second group shot one last time. The black ribbons failed to breach the protective bubble around Esmeray and faded away.

Esmeray laughed a loud, evil laugh and spoke again, "That's it? This was your plan? If you are done with your silly schemes, I will give you another chance to surrender."

Aymelek was now all alone. Without thought, I ran toward her. There was absolutely nothing I could do, but I could not leave her alone with the evil wizard.

Idir and Kratos showed up from the trees and moved toward Aymelek. Then I saw Boris with some guardians join us. We formed a circle around Aymelek as Esmeray's evil laugh echoed through the forest.

She taunted us, "What is going to happen next? I hope you have a better plan than the last one." Behind her, the beast began to move. It was again under Esmeray's control.

All around us, the fire was spreading. It was not an ordinary fire. It burned and ate everything around it quickly. As it spread, the flames grew taller. We were trapped. The fire surrounded us on all sides. In front of us was Esmeray, who was back on the beast.

We looked at each other, wondering what to do. There was no way out.

Esmeray looked directly at Aymelek and hissed, "You dare to think you can defeat me? Savita thought so too. She was too proud to even beg for her life when I dealt with her. I will give you a chance. Side with me, and I will let you live."

Aymelek held her head up. I knew she would never side with the evil wizard. "Do what you can. I am not scared of you." Her voice was calm.

Esmeray continued in her demeaning voice, "And what of this fragile circle of allies around you? Aren't you interested in saving their lives?"

Idir spoke loud enough for Esmeray to hear, "Don't worry about us, Aymelek. We will protect Serenus with our lives."

Esmeray laughed again. "Interesting. You still don't under-stand the danger you are in. Ready to give your life? It's time to teach you a lesson."

Aymelek spoke loudly, "Esmeray! You are not getting the light vials. Elders have already hidden the remaining vials in a safe place. Feray used most of the Moonlight already. Leave now, take what you have and never return."

Esmeray was furious, "How dare you hide the vials. If I can't have the light, no one can."

She let out a deafening shriek. A giant fireball appeared in her hand as she muttered furiously under her breath. It grew bigger and angrier. With pure hatred, she locked her eyes on Aymelek and released the fireball. Aymelek stood rooted to the ground, staring at the burning angel of death rushing toward the Moontree. Fire caught the branches and lit them like dry tinder.

Everyone gasped and ran toward the burning tree. We tried to put out the fire, but it was too furious. Aymelek screamed as the tree started to give up and lose its glow.

Everyone turned to Aymelek with helpless sad eyes. Tears ran down her cheeks in despair. We could only watch the life draining out of the Whitetree.

At this point, no one cared about their own safety. We stood facing the tree with our backs toward Esmeray. Her evil laugh and mockery filled the thick, smoky air around us.

The tree lost all glow quickly, and the light from the Tree Circle around it also grew dull. Suddenly, an idea came to my mind, and I asked everyone to follow me. I ran away from Esmeray and behind the Moontree. Everyone stood there, confused for a moment, and then ran after me, wondering what it was all about.

"Where do you think you are running off to?" Esmeray came after us. As soon as we crossed the Tree Circle, we started running toward the village. Esmeray was now above the Moontree.

Suddenly, the yard lit up, and Esmeray's screams filled the village. We stopped and turned around to witness an incredible scene. The Light trees were glowing brightly, angrily. The Moontree still stood all dark and lifeless. The Violettree had sent a sphere of light up to the sky. Light rays from every tree had rushed to meet the violet sphere. It was a gigantic blacklight bow. It shot shimmering black silk ribbons to attack Esmeray, which wrapped tightly around the struggling wizard and her beast and began to drain them of power to provide for life for the Moontree.

Aymelek was the first to understand what was happening; in the absence of the Moontree light, the other trees drained life from the nearby living things.

We watched in horror as the trees sucked the power out of the wildly shrieking Esmeray. She was still trying to cast a spell to get rid of the black silk gripping her tighter and tighter. She struggled against it, but was no match. The beast fell down with a loud thud, carrying Esmeray with it. Esmeray's screams echoed in the yard, but soon, they diminished to moaning, and then she went quiet. The silk ropes loosened and left Esmeray lying in a heap. The light rays returned to their trees as the Whitetree started to glow again.

For a moment, the yard was calm, except for the crackling of the fire. It, too, had turned into a timid pet abandoned by its master. It slowed down and soon faded away. The spell had lost its potency now that the spell-caster was defeated.

Everyone stayed where they were, waiting. I expected Esmeray to suddenly get up and cast another terrible spell. I had witnessed how powerful she was. Just one spell had left Sere infertile forever. But I had also seen the power of the Lighttrees. Perhaps it was really over this time. I waited along with the others, sweating with uncertainty.

Aymelek went forward cautiously. Everyone followed closely. She bent over Esmeray to check if she was alive. Esmeray stayed still. Aymelek whispered, "She is unconscious." I let out a loud breath of relief.

The light warriors rushed toward her. Boris instructed his guardians to take Esmeray to the waterfall. The guardians dragged the unconscious Esmeray away. Boris went along.

Aymelek went closer to the beast. She walked its length, studying it carefully. Sitting next to it, she closed her eyes for only a moment and then quickly opened them. Her eyes lit up. She asked everyone to move away from her.

We stood near the house, watching and waiting. Aymelek's face became tense as she was struggling with something. Idir went inside the house to inform Alev of the circumstances. She wanted to see what was happening, so two Seren carried her outside in her chair. We waited while Aymelek stayed focused on her work.

A girl came out of the forest. She looked around nervously. Idir called out to her, "Hey, you were supposed to stay away? Why did you come here?" She paused for a moment, then looked at Aymelek, not sure what to say.

Alev called her. "What is it, Luna? Come here." The girl walked to Alev. "Now, tell me, why are you here?"

Luna responded nervously, looking toward Aymelek. "I heard her call. She needs help."

Alev smiled broadly. "Then go and help her."

The girl walked over the burned black ground and went to Aymelek. She sat by her side and closed her eyes. I could see she was focused on something.

"What is happening? Who is she, and how is she helping Aymelek?" It was strange; Aymelek hadn't said a word. But the girl said she heard her call. Why was Alev so happy to see her?

Alev provided the answer. "Aymelek has found her apprentice. She heard her call. I believe that there is still Moonlight left in the beast's body. Aymelek is trying to call it back out of the creature."

Aymelek and her apprentice sat together for some time, then it happened. The body of the beast started to glow with white Moonlight. Slowly, the light left the metal creature and moved up. It was surreal. It seemed like a glowing cloud hovering over the length of the creature's body.

"It is the Moonlight. Quick, Idir! Help them. Get vials from a chamber," Alev said urgently.

We sprinted in different directions, gathering empty vials from the tree chambers, and then took them to Aymelek. Moments later, we walked carefully, carrying the white glowing vials back to the Whitetree.

The creature was left there. It was to be carried to the forge later. Once the sun rose up, Boris came back. Esmeray had been put in the Waterfall Prison. She was still unconscious. He had left some guardians to guard the prison, although there was no fear of her escaping till it was dark. No one was allowed to enter the prison chamber till the elders decided her fate.

It was unbelievable. The worst was over. Boris had already sent one of the guardians to inform the villagers, and they were on their way back. The guardians had put out the fires burning lazily around the yard.

Aymelek and her newly-discovered apprentice were with Alev. She was happy that everything had worked out in the end. But they still needed to decide what to do about Esmeray.

Then there was the case of Feray. No one had any idea what to do about her, either. The matters were left to be discussed later in the evening in the presence of the elders.

The day seemed to go on forever. We tried to rest in the healer's house and waited for the evening.

After resting for a while, we gathered again and went outside to the Tree Circle. There was no fire left, and the Moontree seemed to be recovering by itself. The yard had been cleared away, and the lifeless metal creature was taken to the forge. It was decided that it would be melted down, and the metal would be reused for better purposes.

It was a terrible night, and we still couldn't believe it was over. Still, everyone was worried by Esmeray's presence nearby. We couldn't stop her from escaping once the day ended and the magical barrier of the tree was gone. For now, everyone was trying to focus on the fact that she had been defeated. And what a battle it had been. The Light-trees had surprised everyone. They had stood with us and defended themselves against a powerful enemy.

The elders had gathered for the meeting, but no one was allowed inside. We waited patiently as we looked at the setting sun, worrying that soon, Esmeray could escape again. We had to do something quickly.

Finally, Boris came outside and informed everyone of the decision regarding Esmeray's fate. "Esmeray will be sent into the dark. We cannot take a risk to keep her here." Everyone felt relieved, although it was a terrible ending for Esmeray.

A group of guardians walked to the fall. The entire village followed. Esmeray was awake but very weak. Two guardians carried her, and the procession walked toward the Dark End. Another two guardians brought a boat and put it in the water close to the bank. The guardians put Esmeray in. She protested feebly.

It was apparent that Esmeray was not ready to go into the dark, and, for the first time, she looked scared. She tried to hide her fear and appear strong, but the closer we got to the Dark

End, the more nervous she became. She was no longer a confident, powerful wizard. She had lost her power, but I could see that she was trying to maintain her grace by accepting her fate. Her ability to appear calm even in such a situation surprised me.

The guardians pushed Esmeray's boat to the Dark End as the Seren stood watching. They were finally relieved that the wizard was captured and Serenus had survived a horrible tragedy. The boat moved away. Esmeray looked around, searching for someone. Her eyes stopped at me, and she signaled for me to come closer. I stood motionless as the entire village looked at me.

Kratos held my hand and took me closer to the edge.

Esmeray managed to smile at me. "Listen carefully! I am not the wizard, but he is very fond of you. He has big plans for you. I can't wait to meet you in the next world."

Kratos screamed, "Stop her!" Guardians ran after Esmeray's boat, but with an evil laugh, she crossed the barrier. Soon, she disappeared into the dark.

Boris spoke slowly in shock, "She was not the wizard. But she knew who the wizard was. We should have let Alia interrogate her."

It was no use now. Esmeray was gone, and there was nothing we could do about it. The wizard was still here. We were not safe from danger yet.

Esmeray's last words had disturbed everyone. I felt their eyes on me.

"Finally, we are all safe now." Qilam's voice surprised us. He had come out of the trees and was walking toward us. Guardians ran toward him, but Boris stopped them. There was no point in arresting Qilam now; Esmeray had already been defeated. And there was no doubt that his warnings had proved to be useful after all.

After dinner, I thought of going back home when suddenly, the village bell started to ring. Everyone was startled. The first thought that crossed our minds was that there was another attack. We looked around fearfully but then realized that it was the signal for a newcomer.

Chapter 13

The guardians ran to the river. Others found some torches quickly and went after them. Everyone had a confused look on their face. Kratos came to my side and said, "We need to go. Something is not right."

"What do you mean?" I asked. He pulled me away and said, "Esmeray just left, and a newcomer is coming. Haven't you heard that the wizard cannot be killed and always comes back? I think she was lying. She must be the wizard. Now, she is back in yet another disguise to torment us."

He looked worried as he continued, "She singled you out. I think you could be in danger."

Aymelek ran toward the fall, holding her notebook. I turned to Kratos and said, "Let's go see who it is." Kratos was worried, but I insisted that there was nothing to worry about. It wasn't as if the newcomer would attack me the moment we saw each other. He called Idir, and together we headed to the river.

Once there, a strange scene unfolded, and I couldn't believe my eyes. The newcomer had not yet landed. Clouds covered the moon but he was clearly visible, standing tall in his boat, holding the paper with the poem on it. Standing in a boat that everyone was scared of sitting in, his wings spread out behind him, balancing him in the rocking boat effortlessly. His left hand was on the hip and in his right hand, he was holding the poem in front of him. He had a look of confidence and authority. He glanced at everyone waiting for him to reach the land without concern and was not unnerved as he spotted the waterfall.

The Seren were so shocked to see him that no one went forward to help him with his boat. Even the guardians stood back, uncertain of what they were supposed to do. He jumped out without looking back at his boat and landed slowly on the sand as his wings slowed his fall. The waves carried his boat toward the waterfall, and it smashed into the rocks and broke into pieces. The current carried the shattered fragments to the edge, where they fell over. The newcomer didn't even look at it.

He stood motionless as he stepped on the land. It was as if he were assessing something in his mind. A slow smile spread across his face, and he gave a single nod. He was happy with whatever he had found. Then, he lifted his hand, holding the paper, and waved it in front of us. "Where is the wizard?" Then he pointed to the fall and said, "Is that the fall we are supposed to go past?"

Everyone was stunned by his words. No one answered.

Aymelek hesitated for a moment, then she went close, carefully. The newcomer watched her with interest. "Newcomer! I welcome you on behalf of everyone here."

"What is here?" he asked.

"This is Serenus, the land of peace, and we are Seren. You

are too. From now on, you will be living here with us. But first—"

"I have no such intention," he interrupted her.

Aymelek was stumped. For a moment, she lost her composure and looked at Boris helplessly. Boris nodded to her and went closer.

We were all puzzled and impressed by the newcomer's confidence.

Boris faced the newcomer. "You need to come with us."

"Why and where?" He was uncomfortably straightforward.

Boris pointed toward the waterfall. "There is a tree on a small island under the waterfalls. Once you get there, we will answer your questions."

I didn't expect the newcomer to agree. I was sure he would want to know why he should go there. But he nodded and said in an amused tone, "Fair enough!"

Without any effort, he spread his wings and, with a powerful thrust, flew high above the ground. We watched him, mouths ajar as he reached the waterfall, hovered above it to study the island, and then dove down with his wings pinned to his body. Everyone ran toward the waterfall. I was sure he would have made a perfect landing on the island. I wished I could get there before he landed. I really wanted to see it with my own eyes. Sure enough, he was standing next to the tree when I reached the edge.

Boris asked everyone to stay back. We didn't know anything about the newcomer. It was better to take precautions. He continued down the side of the falls. Aymelek, Kratos, and three guardians followed them. They approached him carefully. It was difficult to see their faces in the Moonlight from this far, but I could visualize their uncertain faces. I regretted that I hadn't asked Kratos if I could go with them.

They exchanged some words, but the newcomer didn't move toward the tree. Instead, he took a step back. The guardians charged at him and pointed their spears at him, apparently threatening him. It was clear he had refused to go into the tree chamber. Everyone was anxious.

I could see that Aymelek, Kratos, and Boris were talking to him, but there was no change in his stance. Suddenly, one of the guardians moved forward with his spear extended toward him.

The newcomer turned toward the guardian and spread his arms in front of him. The guardian stopped where he was and fell down, lying motionless on the ground. Others moved back, afraid to attack him.

The Seren gasped in fear and started moving away from the edge. The newcomer had magic. I broke into a cold sweat. Esmeray had lied to us. She was the wizard, and as she had left the island, another one had arrived to take her place. I was worried for my friends who were so close to him.

Kratos and Boris had covered Aymelek and were facing the wizard, though it was beyond me what they could do to fight him. But the newcomer didn't advance toward them. He stood there, watching them for some time, and then spread his wings and flew away toward the dark forest.

I relaxed a little, breathing deeply now that the wizard had left. I looked around me and was shocked to see that I was standing alone on the ledge. Everyone had run away to the village.

I left all caution and ran down. My friends had gathered around the poor guard. I was relieved to know that he was still breathing.

Boris shouted orders to the guardians, who helped carry their fellow and climbed up the path as quickly as possible. Aymelek left with them as the guardian needed help immediately. He was taken to the Tree Circle.

I followed Kratos and Boris back to the village. I was aching to know what had happened. The strained faces of my friends worried me. On my inquiry, Boris responded, "We are in trouble. Let's go inform the elders."

The news had traveled fast. We didn't see anyone except the guardians on our way back, who stood alert and tense. The Seren were scared and sought the safety of their homes. A deadly silence held the village in its cruel clutches.

My company was equally tense. No one said anything till we arrived at the healer's home. The elders were already there. It had become a permanent meeting place during desperate times. We had to wait for Aymelek to arrive. When she informed us that the guardian would live, everyone breathed a sigh of relief.

Then, Boris briefed the elders as we listened to him in silence. He told us what had happened on the island under the fall. "The newcomer refused to go in. We tried our best to persuade him, but he wouldn't listen."

Aymelek continued, "I believe that he could somehow sense the tree was magical. When the guardian threatened to attack him, he used magic. It was not a simple spell. The wizard had thought it out in a fraction of a moment. He didn't intend to kill. If he had, the guardian would have had no chance."

She looked at us with horror in her eyes. "He is nothing like the wizards we have faced before. He is extremely powerful. His mind is sharp and calculating. You saw how he had already decided what he would do—catch the wizard and go past the falls. People take a lifetime to arrive at such conclusions. He knew he could fly. He knew we couldn't hurt him. He knows his powers. That makes him extremely dangerous."

Alev put her head in her hands. I was surprised to see her like that. Despite her years, she had always been composed and in control. Jinyan went and sat next to her. He addressed her gently, "Alev! Don't let him take your courage away. The Seren rely on your strength. It would break their spirit if they saw you like this."

Alev slowly raised her head, nodded at him, and pulled herself together. "You are right, Jinyan. This is not the time to lose ourselves. Aymelek, what do you—"

An urgent knock at the door stopped her in mid-sentence. Boris opened the door and let in a guardian. He looked pretty unnerved.

"What happened, Aylan?" Boris enquired.

"The newcomer! He is dangerous. I believe he is the wizard. I don't know how to explain it. I have just been to the river where he landed. I was supposed to patrol that area, and I saw something there." He shuddered as he tried to explain.

"What did you see, Aylan? Tell us," Alev said, agitated.

Aylan looked at us in fear. "I saw a small area on the river bank that is shaped like a footprint. I believe it is where the newcomer put his first step on the land. The grass in that place is badly burned."

The room went silent. We looked at each other helplessly. None of us had a clue what we were going to do.

Finally, Alev said, "Boris! Place your guardians everywhere around the village and the Tree Circle. We must protect Serenus." Then, she turned to Kratos. "Take No Name with you. Tell everyone to stay inside. No one is allowed to leave their houses."

She asked Aymelek to stay behind while some guardians accompanied the elders to the safety of their homes. Kratos and I got up and left quickly. Misa and Fabio were waiting outside with Idir. Kratos briefed them about Alev's orders. Boris and Aylan went to the guardians as we left for the village. Everyone kept looking around cautiously. The wizard was unpredictable and dangerous. The sounds of the night added to the anxious atmosphere.

We went from door to door, advising Seren to stay inside no matter what. Everyone was on edge and wanted to know how we would deal with the new wizard. We had no words to console them. The uncertainty fuelled their fears. By the time we left the last home, we were exhausted.

Now that we were close to my house, I invited everyone to rest for a while. They nodded in agreement, and we moved forward in silence.

I felt safer sitting in front of the roaring fire in my fireplace, surrounded by my friends. But I knew it was not permanent. No one was safe anymore. Nothing was certain.

Defeating Esmeray had given everyone confidence that we were not helpless after all. We had captured her and sent her into the dark. But the coming of a new wizard had shattered it completely. My mind kept bringing back the image of the guardian lying motionless on the ground. I felt entirely helpless.

When I couldn't take it anymore, I voiced my fears to my friends. "What will we do now? He is too powerful. And we can't do anything."

Kratos rushed to my side and held my hands firmly. "We will stop him. Together, we will find a way. Don't lose yourself to this fear, my friend! We are here with you. Don't give up." He looked at others and spoke firmly, "Listen to me, all of you! I do not allow anyone to give up. Don't waste your energy on being afraid and worried. Use it for thinking of ways we could deal with him. We are here to give courage to our fellows, not break their spirit. Look up, Fabio! Pull yourself together."

His words made me feel better. He had scolded us like an elder. It felt good. I felt loved. So did the others. We sat up and gathered our nerves.

"That's more like it. Now, let's go back and see what Aymelek and Alev have been thinking." Kratos stood up and patted my shoulder. I nodded and got up. We left home with renewed spirits. The walk back to the healer's house was not scary anymore.

Aymelek and Alev were sitting silently in the healer's house. They had been discussing the newcomer, but it seemed that we couldn't get much information about him from our short encounter. Still, Alev wanted us to discuss it once again. She asked Aymelek to tell us what she thought about the new wizard.

"Well, we know that the newcomer has magic unlike we have seen before. He is a quick learner. He has already learned how to fly and use his magical powers. He knows he is more powerful and stronger than all of us. We gave that away, ourselves." She shook her head, expressing her disapproval. "We acted without thinking—how timid we must have seemed when we let him see how impressed we were by his abilities."

Everyone was embarrassed by her words, but she was right. Aymelek continued, "Never in the known history has a newcomer arrived here at night. I have no idea what it means. Should we be worried about it, or is it just an unusual but perfectly normal arrival? But then there is Aylan's information about what he witnessed at the river bank. I can't say anything about it without studying the area. There is so little that we know. And what we do know is enough to scare us. Still, there is something that gives me hope."

She paused. I wondered what it could be. Everyone watched, curious. Alev leaned forward in her chair to listen to what Aymelek had to say.

"The new wizard is focused on going past the falls. It is possible that he won't disturb us and leave soon." Aymelek's words felt like fresh air in the suffocating atmosphere of hopelessness and depression. Everyone sat up with their faces lit. She could be right. The new wizard might not be as troublesome and dangerous as we thought.

Something nudged me at the back of my mind. I tried to figure out what was bothering me. The newcomer's words rang in my mind, and I realized we were wrong. Or we might be. I cleared my throat and repeated his words loudly, "Where is the wizard?"

Everyone turned toward me, watching me in surprised confusion. "Where is the wizard? Those were the words of the newcomer when he arrived. If he is the new wizard, why did he ask that? He is not afraid of us, so he had no reason to pretend that he wasn't the new wizard. On the contrary, I believe, if he was the one, he would have said that without any fear or care."

Idir nodded. "You are right. We assumed that he was the new wizard just because he had magic. No doubt, he is a wizard, but we can't be sure if he came to replace Esmeray."

"That brings us back to an Esmeray situation. We have another powerful wizard who wants to go past the falls. What we don't know is if he would simply leave or cause trouble." Aymelek paused. Her voice reflected her worry when she continued, "I hope he doesn't become greedy. How would we stop him if he came after the vials?"

Alev tried to comfort everyone and said, "Don't forget the Blacklight bows. They helped us deal with Esmeray. And what about the Lighttrees? It's not like our hands are empty."

Boris interjected, "I think we should go after him with Blacklight bows and be done with this uncertainty. Why wait for him to attack. Even if he is not the wizard we have to capture, we know he is dangerous. I say we should go for it."

Alev shook her head forcefully. "No, Boris, we don't have enough light for bows, and I don't think it is wise to invite trouble. We have already mishandled the first encounter with the newcomer. I don't want anyone to go after him without bringing it to our knowledge."

Kratos said, "Alev is right. Serenus will protect itself if need be. We should wait and see what this new wizard is up to. If he leaves without causing trouble, great. If not, we will find a way to deal with him as well."

Everyone agreed to wait and see.

We had missed the better part of the night. Alev asked everyone to rest. She was staying at the healer's home with Aymelek. Misa and Fabio offered to stay with them. Kratos invited Idir and me to his house. On hearing this, Alev remembered something: "We are forgetting something. Remember Esmeray's last words? If the newcomer is the wizard by any chance, this one could be in danger. We don't know what Esmeray meant by the wizard's plan about this one." She paused and scolded me, "For light's sake, pick a name already."

I bent my head down. She sighed loudly and said, "Boris, put two guardians at the lodge. We can't leave him alone at his house. He will stay at the lodge till we find out more."

Kratos and Idir stayed with me at the Serenus Lodge. They

didn't want to leave me alone. The moment I lay down in bed, I realized how exhausted I was.

I fell asleep immediately and woke up to the thunderous voice of Idir. I sat up with a start. Idir was standing next to my bed. "Goodness! Is this how you sleep? I have been trying to wake you up for ages. Get up now. We need to go check the footprint on the river bank."

His words jolted me out of sleep, and I got up. Idir told me that Aymelek had visited earlier, and Kratos had gone to the river with her.

We had a quick breakfast, and left for the river. The village was silent and deserted. No one wandered outside except for the guardians walking around with spears in their hands.

We found Kratos and Aymelek sitting at the riverbank, studying the footprint. I went closer to see. It was exactly as Aylan had described.

Aymelek pulled out some grass using metal tongs. We gasped as we saw that it had been charred to the very roots.

"What happened here, Aymelek?" Kratos wanted to know her views on the matter.

Aymelek replied thoughtfully, "I don't know for sure, but I think the new wizard sucked the energy out of the grass when he stepped on it. That's the only explanation for this condition of the grass."

I added, "The newcomer stopped when he stepped on the ground. I am sure all of you noticed how he smiled at the time.

I think he had drained the life out of the grass without intention. But the very next moment, he realized what had happened." Everyone nodded in agreement.

"We should visit the tree under the fall as well. If the newcomer had taken energy from the grass, we might find more burnt grass there as he had used his magic on a guardian there." I suggested.

"Good thinking!" Kratos replied, "Let's go and check."

My doubts proved to be correct. The grass was burned in some places near the tree on the island. Fortunately, the tree was safe. Though one area of burned grass extended right underneath its tresses and into the tree chamber.

The matter worried us greatly. Aymelek's idea seemed to be right. The newcomer had the power to drain the life out of the grass. Once again, we decided to talk to the elders.

The elders were anxious to hear what Aymelek had to say. Jinyan asked, "Does it mean that the newcomer can drain the life out of other living things as well?"

"I don't know. But it is not impossible, either. We will have to wait and see," Aymelek replied.

Chapter 14

Icontinued to stay at the lodge. Kratos and Idir visited me often and gave me company. These were difficult times, and the Seren felt imprisoned in their own homes. The village center was deserted, and the laughter and pleasant conversations that filled it became a thing of the past. The guardians took provisions to every villager.

We were waiting for the new wizard to do something—anything—so we could get more information about him and his plans. He was seen many times, flying over the island. But he hadn't shown any interest in the village.

Gradually, we started to feel that the newcomer wasn't planning to come to the village and harm anyone. Waiting was difficult and had started to affect the Seren. Everyone became short-tempered and frustrated.

The elders decided to lift the curfew after a week. The Seren were still advised to stay closer to the village while the guardians were spread around the village borders.

People were happy to get out of their homes finally. The atmosphere was still tense, but it had improved. The elders ordered everyone to take turns to visit the Tree Circle to dissolve the effects of the curfew.

I visited the healer's home with Kratos and Idir. The elders had moved there as well. They were going to remain till we resolved the situation. I had not seen Aymelek in a while, and she wasn't at the healer's house, so I went to the Tree Circle looking for her. I found her under the Yellowtree, which surprised me. She was clearly troubled by her thoughts, but the Yellowtree was not the right place to be in such a situation.

I sat by her silently. In a little bit, Aymelek started speaking, "Ever since Alfred left through the Dark End, I have thought of going after him. He might be alone there, waiting for me. I wanted to be a good student with Feray, but she deserted and deceived me. My work with the trees is always under attack. I don't think I have any chance of a happy life on this island."

I had never expected to hear these words from Aymelek. Now I realized that I didn't really know how depressed she was. I tried to remind her that she had told me it was a foolish idea to go in search of more islands.

"Maybe there isn't another land, but maybe there is, and Alfred is waiting for me, hoping and praying that I will go after him? There is no way of knowing until I go to find out." Aymelek had been seriously thinking about going into the Dark End. Her thoughts scared me.

I begged, "Aymelek, promise me you will never do such a thing. And if you did, I will try to stop you, and if I fail, I will follow you. If we ever leave, we will leave together."

Aymelek smiled and said, "Let's go together."

Once again, I was shocked by what she was saying. "What's

happened to you? Why are you saying such things? Everything will be okay. We will deal with the wizard just like we dealt with Esmeray. We will find a way."

The Yellowtree was creating strange thoughts in her mind. I convinced her to go to the Greentree, and we both sat there for some time. I felt much clearer in my mind now and felt a change in Aymelek's look too. She smiled embarrassingly and said, "I'm sorry if I freaked you out."

I laughed and said, "It's okay. It was the Yellowtree doing the talking, not you."

Aymelek stayed for a while and then left to get back to her work. I thought about how powerful the effects of the tree were. They could temporarily change the whole personality of a person.

I decided to stay a bit longer and think about the poem. I cleared my mind and focused on its meaning, but even after several attempts, I failed to reach the mental state where I could keep thinking about a matter with conviction and clarity. The tree did not seem to be helping.

I tried again and thought about the words literally and figuratively, but without help from the tree, the more I thought, the more ambiguous it felt. As if whoever gave us the poem did not want us to find out what the words meant. The only thing I could say with some level of certainty was that we had a limited amount of time to do something, maybe to understand the poem? If catching the wizard and going past the fall was not the objective, then what else could it be? And what was the fruitless war? Was it the forever war between the wizard and the villagers? If it was futile, then why did the poem tell us to catch the wizard in the first place? And how were we supposed to find out in our past that our world was vast?

Next, I thought about Qilam's poem. If he told the truth that he came with it, could it help me understand my poem? The words "beyond this earth" did seem to imply that there could be more islands ahead of us. Maybe the story of the lost scroll was true. Would the finder of the lost scroll become a god beyond this earth? But were we supposed to find it on this island and then proceed, or were we supposed to look for it on the subsequent islands? Then I remembered the line that said it didn't matter if we failed. Why not? Nothing made sense, and I stopped myself from thinking along this line because if we needed Qilam's poem to solve the riddle, why wasn't it given to others? It was more likely that Qilam was lying about it.

In the end, I concluded that if this poem was a prophecy, it really was clever, cruel, and tiring; a mystery without clues and even the tree did not want to help with it.

I left the Green chamber and met Fabio and Misa. We chatted for a while, grateful for each other's company. Everyone avoided talking about the new wizard as it only brought worry. After catching up, we went to the village center for the midday meal.

I had not expected to see the village center so full. It was not bustling with joy and laughter as it used to be, but it seemed that every Seren had come to be with their friends. We sat together and ate our lunch, talking in low voices. No one spoke about the wizard, but he was on everyone's mind. We kept looking around with cautious eyes, and any unexpected sound caused our heartbeats to race. The wizard had destroyed the peace of Serenus. I wished we could go back to the Serenus of the past when all I had to worry about was finding a question that interested me.

As the days passed, we relaxed and got busy with our routine life. We would have thought that the wizard had left the island if we hadn't found the occasional signs of his presence. Mostly, it was the woodworkers who brought the news of areas of land and plants burnt in places. No one had ever found any animal burned or dead. It meant that the wizard could only take the energy from grass, plants, and trees. The realization raised our spirits.

Gradually, Serenus returned to normal. Once again, the village center echoed with laughter and merry chitchat. Seren still talked about the wizard occasionally, but he had lost his effect on them.

Kratos and Idir had already moved back to their homes. I felt bored at the Serenus Lodge. Eventually, I begged the elders to let me go back to my house.

Three weeks after the arrival of the newcomer, I returned home. Kratos and Idir came with me. I was devastated to see the condition of my house and the yards. Fallen leaves had covered every possible place around my house. Autumn was here. I wanted to clean my yard before the snow came. It took a day's hard work to get rid of the leaves. Kratos and Idir helped with the cleaning.

We stayed up late at night and chatted happily. Kratos

reminded me to plant some flowering bushes in the yard. I had planned to do so but hadn't found the time. Idir reminded me about the pet I had wanted to adopt. I wasn't sure anymore but said I would think about it.

I slept peacefully, happy to be home. Early next morning, Kratos and Idir left for the forge, and I was alone at my home.

I quickly finished some chores, then picked a paper and pen and sat down comfortably. I wrote down everything we knew about the wizard and whatever we thought about him and his abilities. He had been on my mind from the moment he had arrived. There were so many questions that needed answers, but I had no way to find out. It frustrated me.

I thought about a way to find answers and came up with a plan. The first step was already complete; I was back at my home. The next step needed courage as well as luck. But I had decided to get on with it no matter what. After thinking for a long time, I put the paper and pen away and went to the village center for lunch. I didn't meet my friends there. I thought they must be at the forge because, over the past several weeks, a lot of work had piled up there. After lunch, I gathered provisions and returned home.

After leaving my firewood and food at home, I left for the trail in the forest in search of Qilam. I was sure he would know things about the wizard that we didn't. He always did. Surprisingly, I found him at the same place where I had met him the first time. For some reason, he looked delighted to see me. We sat together on a fallen log, and he asked me about the village. I told him how everything was back to normal. Then, I asked him what he knew about the wizard.

He laughed and replied, "Why don't you ask the wizard yourself?"

Right then, the wizard appeared out of the trees. I was shocked to see him so unexpectedly. Esmeray's words rang in my head. Had I walked into my death trap all by myself? There was no one to protect me. My friends didn't even know I was here. I regretted visiting Qilam, but there was nothing to do now. I was there. The wizard walked up to me and stood facing me.

"What happened, Thinker? Why are you scared?" he asked in a casual tone. He knew who I was. I guessed Qilam must have told him.

I gathered myself and replied, "I am scared of the unknown. Who knows what you are capable of?"

He laughed. "I am quite capable, but not insane. I won't hurt anyone without reason."

"You hurt the guardian the day you came here, and I have heard that you drain the life out of living things. These are not insane actions? I have reason to think that you are dangerous."

My answer amused the wizard. He sat down on the grass and invited me to sit with him. "You are not thinking proper-ly. Do you know why? Because you are sitting on a dead tree. These trees, plants, and this grass are pulsating with energy. You stay close to them, and they share their energy with you. The dead ones will only drain you. I have been telling the same thing to Qilam, but apparently, he has been sitting on dead trees for far too long. His mind doesn't understand the very basic concepts."

Qilam laughed heartily at his words. I left the log and sat down with him cautiously. He continued, "Yes, I have powers, and I hurt the guardian, but he tried to attack first. I take energy from the things around me because they are there for that very purpose. So, if you've come in peace, you have no reason to think I am dangerous."

I was surprised at how casually he spoke to me. I considered him a grave threat, but he talked to me as normally as anyone in Serenus would. He had a dark sense of humor as well.

I relaxed a little and decided to probe further to know him better. As if reading my thoughts, he asked me, "What do you want to know about me, Thinker? Qilam says you are good at asking questions. Let me see if you are good enough."

"Why are you here?" I started with the simplest one.

"I am here because I was sent. I have a mission, and I must complete it." He shrugged.

"So, you think the poem tells us about our mission?"

"There is no reason to think otherwise. Even Qilam can understand it. He told me that everyone came here in the same way with the same instructions. I wonder why they have started to live here as if this is their final destination. Not that it's my concern, but we must go past the falls. I have seen Qilam's poem too. I know you read it—"

"You trust what Qilam says? What if he is tricking us into

believing that he had that poem with him? What if he wrote it himself?"

Qilam cleared his throat loudly to remind me that he was right there. I ignored him.

The wizard laughed. "See Qilam! It's not just me who doesn't believe you." Then he added in a serious tone, "Qilam can be manipulative, but I believe he is not lying about the poem because it makes sense."

I asked directly, "So, what are your plans, then?"

"Straight to the point, huh? I like it. I am here on a mission. Going past the falls is the next most significant task because it needs courage and blind faith. Whoever sent me here wants me to follow the instructions, and those who will do what they want will be rewarded. I am more powerful than the rest, so I have the best chance of success."

"Qilam claims to have understood this for a long time, but he is still here. Do you have blind faith in this interpretation?" I saw Qilam drop his head, staring at his feet in embarrassment.

The wizard replied, "Qilam is a coward. Success in the mission is the only thing that matters. If I don't try it, what else is there to do in this world?"

I highlighted the weakness in his understanding. "But you forgot one thing. Before going past the falls, we need to capture the wizard. The Seren have done that repeatedly, but he reappears every time they kill him or send him into the Dark End. How can we go past the falls if the wizard is always here?"

The newcomer laughed, shaking his head. "Thinker, you have not thought about these lines yet. If you had, you would know that no one was supposed to catch the wizard who lives here. Now listen carefully. Every one of us is different and has a unique set of abilities. If the ability is complex to understand, you call it magical, but to me, you are a bigger wizard than Esmeray ever was. Thinking is an ability that I wouldn't claim to understand. Every one of us is a wizard. 'Catch the wizard' simply means to explore those abilities to find the wizard in us. To find ourselves, and then go past the falls with full preparation."

I understood what he was trying to say. I acknowledged it to keep the conversation going in the direction that provided me the answers I needed. "Hmm, people took the poem literally and focussed on capturing the wizard instead of trying to understand themselves and their abilities."

"Exactly. Now you understand. I feel like I have been wasting time with the wrong companion." He winked at Qilam teasingly.

His mindset was becoming clearer and clearer, but I needed to know if his plans could threaten the village. I probed on, "But now that you know about your powers and have gained more, why haven't you left the island?"

"Not yet. There is something I need to do. When I arrived here, I could feel the magic vibrating in the very air of the island. Over time, I learned to gather this power inside me. As I grew powerful, my senses became sharper. I could feel which plants or trees had more magic. So, instead of wasting my time on the ones that couldn't give me much, I focused on the ones that gave me more power. Look at that tree." He pointed at a tree right behind Qilam. "It is bursting with energy. Let me show you."

He got up and walked toward the tree.

Qilam shouted at him, "Stop it. I told you not to do it around my place."

He shrugged his protest away. "Qilam, don't be stupid. It's a waste of energy."

He put his hand on the tree trunk. The moment he touched it, the tree began to glow. Slowly, the light started to move toward the wizard's hand, and the glow transferred to his body as the light absorbed into it. The tree began to shrink and wither. The wizard moved away from it. The tree twisted and turned as if being burnt in an invisible fire. It was terrifying and very unnatural to see a tree dying like that.

Qilam and I saw the terrible scene with horror. The wizard walked toward us as if nothing had happened. But I couldn't take my eyes off the tree.

"This is not right. The tree was alive, and you killed it for no reason." My voice was a mere whisper.

The wizard was not affected by my emotions. He responded, "Everything is a means to an end. The boat was there to bring us here. The poem was there to tell us about the mission. This tree was there to provide me with power. Everything on this island is here for us to take, to prepare us for the next step. There is nothing to be sad about."

"That's cruel," I protested.

"No, not at all. Don't the villagers cut down trees to build homes with the wood? If I had taken its energy without really needing it, it would have been cruel. If I had killed it for pleasure, it would have been cruel. If I waste the power I have taken, it would be cruel, but I have no such intentions. I am not here to hurt anyone. I am simply taking what is needed for my mission. The ones who sent me here gave me this mission and put this tree here. They grew it for a purpose. So, there is nothing wrong with taking what is needed."

"How do you know what you need for your mission?" I was upset and no longer interested in encouraging the conversation.

"Well, that's what I have understood from the poem. My mission is to gather power, increase my abilities, and go to the next world. How much do I need, and exactly how I would use it? I don't know. That will come later in the next world. Right now, I need to gather as much power as possible. I would like to take it all, but then it would take a really long time, and as you know, we shouldn't stall…."

I had a much better understanding of the person standing in front of me. We were right to think that the wizard could be very dangerous. He had a justification for his actions but no morality or guiding compass to judge it with. If he felt it was needed for his mission, he could hurt anyone, and he would do it without any remorse.

The wizard walked away, leaving me alone in my miserable realization. Qilam muttered something inaudible and followed him. The tree behind him was still suffering. I had seen how casually the wizard had snatched a life. His twisted thoughts scared me.

I was wrong to think that I was controlling the direction of our conversation. I felt guilty for leading him on and could no longer stay in the presence of the dying tree. I turned and ran out of there, and kept running till I reached my home. I waited by the front door, trying to catch my breath. When I could breathe again, I turned around, opened the door, went inside, and screamed loudly in frustration.

I didn't realize that there was someone there, facing the fireplace. My screams startled him, and he turned around in shock.

It was Kratos, looking at me with concern. Seeing him relieved me. He helped me to a chair and asked what had happened. For some time, I couldn't speak. Kratos brought me a glass of water and asked me to relax. I told him everything as soon as I could talk. His eyes went wide as I told him how the wizard killed the tree. Then, I realized that the wizard had not told me why he hadn't left the island. He was about to tell me, but I was so affected by the killing of the tree that I didn't get the chance to press him.

Kratos was beyond worry. He wanted me to inform the elders about what I had learned about the wizard. But I wanted to discuss it with Aymelek. He agreed, but since it was getting dark, he invited me to stay with him for the night. He was unwilling to let me come back home late at night.

We left for the Tree Circle, hoping to find Aymelek there. She was in the Yellowtree with Luna, her apprentice. She was teaching her about the effects of the Yellowlight. Kratos and I sat down with them, pretending that we were just there to see her.

"The Yellowlight is quite interesting. When the Seren sit in the yellow chamber, they experience a boost in their imagination. It is better to visit the green chamber afterward to bring clarity to your thoughts."

We waited patiently as Aymelek went on and on, describing its properties to Luna. Kratos and I sighed in relief when Aymelek finished and Luna left.

She eyed us suspiciously. "What happened?"

"We need to talk, but not here. Somewhere alone," I explained.

"Well, alright. But you know, the elders are here at my home."

"Let's go to my home, then. I am not expecting anyone today—it's safe there. Both of you can stay for the night." Kratos solved the problem, and we went to the village center together. After dinner, we walked briskly to Kratos's house. He built up a roaring fire while I made tea, and we sat down around the fire. It was a freezing cold night.

I narrated everything that had happened in detail. Aymelek listened intently. Her face contorted with disgust when I recounted how casually the wizard had killed the tree. When I finished, Kratos asked her if it was true. Did all the trees, plants, and grass have magic like the Lighttrees? She stayed quiet, thinking. Then, she started speaking slowly.

"I have never seen or heard anything like that. But since our thinker friend has seen it with his eyes, it must be so. I have never felt the magic in any other tree except the Lighttrees. But the wizard may have the power to feel it. He is very different from the ones we have dealt with in the past. I am afraid I don't understand his powers at all."

"Now what? Where does this leave us, then?" I asked.

"I think if he told the truth," Kratos said, "and I believe he did, he has no intention of hurting anyone. He doesn't need anything from us. I think once he has collected enough power, he will leave. Though the thought of him destroying the trees disgusts me, there is nothing that we can do to stop him. But I definitely want to know the reason why he doesn't leave."

"The reason is quite obvious—he is after the Tree Circle." Aymelek leaned forward. Her eyes reflected fear. "It is only a matter of time. He has seen the tree under the fall. Remember? He could sense its magic. He must have felt the presence of the Tree Circle as well. It is the most powerful source of power on this island, and he will definitely come for it."

She fell silent. Kratos stood up and started pacing. The situation was grave. We had no means to fight the wizard. We didn't even know much about his capabilities. But one thing was clear—he was not to be taken lightly.

"What should we do now?" I asked. "We have seen that the Blacklight bows couldn't do much to defeat Esmeray. This wizard is much more powerful than her. And I am sure he won't stop no matter what."

Aymelek interrupted me, "We will find a way—we have to. If the Tree Circle dies, there is no telling what would happen. I am afraid Serenus wouldn't be able to survive without them."

"The elders might think of something. We will tell them in the morning. I am sure, together, we'll find a way." Kratos tried to ease our fears, but I could see how worried he was.

We stayed awake for a long time, thinking about a way out of this trouble, but no one came up with anything. There seemed to be nothing we could do, but we couldn't give up either. I was so exhausted and anxious that I couldn't even think straight. Finally, we decided to rest. I fell asleep thinking about ways to defend Serenus.

***

It was bright and sunny when I walked to the village center and stood by a tree with an empty mind, enjoying the warmth of the sun. After a few moments, my attention diverted to a Seren walking between the benches. It startled me when I realized that it was the wizard right here in the village center, pacing around worry-free. Everyone was watching him with fearful eyes. As he walked among them, the Seren cringed away from him.

The wizard turned around and came to stand right in front of me and spoke in a cold, menacing voice, "I can feel a presence here. More powerful than any I have found yet. It taunts me, but I can't sense exactly where it is. Do you know what it could be?"

His words fell on my ears like daggers. I knew what it was,

but I could never tell him. I feigned ignorance.

The wizard nodded dangerously.

He walked to the nearest table, where Aymelek and Kratos were sitting together. He grabbed Aymelek and dragged her back to me. Kratos and I froze and watched in horror. Aymelek's eyes bulged out in fear. She didn't make any sound, but I could see her eyes pleading with me to save her. I tried to move, but my body refused to respond. I stood rooted to the ground.

The wizard left Aymelek. She fell down at my feet. Then, he raised his hands, and she rose up in the air like a doll. Her body went limp. I wanted to scream, but all I could do was whimper inaudibly.

The wizard said, "Thinker! Don't you love your friends? You know I don't want to hurt them, but what can I do? You deny me what I need. Tell me where it is, and I will leave her alone."

My eyes were fixed on an unconscious Aymelek. Inside my head, a battle raged. Tree Circle or Aymelek? Who should I choose? Suddenly, Aymelek opened her eyes and looked at me with a dead, emotionless stare. I broke into a cold sweat. The battle inside me turned vicious. A small voice hiding some-where in my mind whispered, "Friend."

As if under someone's control, I lifted my hand slowly and pointed toward the trees, and whispered, "The Tree Circle."

Aymelek came back to life and screamed. The Seren got up and started running away. The wizard released Aymelek, and with a powerful thrust, flew away toward the Tree Circle. She fell to the ground. I rushed to her, but she pushed me away, screaming wildly. She got up and ran after the wizard. I followed her.

The wizard landed next to the Tree Circle and began to walk around it, studying it in a calculating way. The Seren stood watching him from a distance.

Aymelek and I reached the wizard and tried to tackle him to the ground. He was very still, laughing a vicious evil laugh. For all our effort, we couldn't even move him one bit. He seemed entertained by our desperate attempts to stop him and continued to laugh mockingly.

Suddenly, the wizard's face changed into Esmeray, then back to his own, and they laughed together, transforming into each other repeatedly.

I remembered Esmeray's attack on the Moontree. The village bells were ringing, but there was no fire this time except the one burning inside us. This wizard was too strong to stop.

Finally, the wizard walked forward, dragging us with him. Then, his wings spread out and, with a powerful thrust, left us on the ground and flew to the Moontree. I ran frantically to the healer's home and found the Blacklight bows. I picked one, ran back to the Tree Circle, and pointed it to the wizard. Black silk ribbons lunged at the wizard and covered him completely.

For a moment, I thought it had the wizard under control, but he rotated his hand around the ribbons and held the silk. I waited for him to get weaker but saw a smile appear on his face. His body started to glow, and he began to grow in size as he absorbed the silk that fell on him.

It was too late when I realized my mistake. The wizard could drain all power and absorb it, making him stronger. I threw the bow away, but the shimmering silk didn't fade till he pulled all light out of the vials.

I looked at Aymelek. She was sitting on the ground, watching in despair, so powerless that she was not even thinking of trying to stop him anymore - just watching him with a blank stare.

The wizard was now twice my size, becoming a mighty giant, still growing. If one bow could give him this much power, what kind of power could the entire Tree Circle and all the lights inside them give him? I fell to the ground in defeat.

Kratos and Idir came and stood next to me. Their eyes fixed on the tragedy that befell us. Behind us, the whole village stood silently. We watched helplessly as the wizard walked to the Moontree and grabbed the glowing white tresses with both hands.

The Moontree began to glow brightly, and the light started to flow through the tresses into the wizard's body, making it shine brighter and brighter till our eyes couldn't look anymore. The Tree Circle faded. I sat helplessly, covering my eyes with my hand, trying to peek at the blinding white.

The wizard let out continuous screams of joy. They became louder and louder. I felt pain in my ears as they grew more horrifying.

I wanted to understand what was happening, but his body was only a bright orb. It was hard to see. I looked at the aura that formed his arms and sensed he was pulling his arms back. Was he done draining all light out of the circle? Suddenly, and with a jerk, the tree pulled him back toward it. They were locked in a tight embrace, and the wizard struggled, but the tree wouldn't let him go.

The Moontree started to wrap its tresses around the wizard's body. It twisted his arms and crushed his legs as he struggled against their clutches in vain. His screams went lower and lower, and the orb turned even brighter. I turned away from it, unable to take its intensity.

The wizard screamed one last light time. I turned around and tried to look at him with squinted eyes. With a loud bang, he burst into an explosion of energy that spread everywhere before it faded away.

Someone shook me violently. I sat up with a start and opened my eyes. Kratos stood next to me with a worried face. I was sweating profusely. Aymelek rushed to me and gave me some water. It took me some time to understand what had happened. I sighed in relief and fell back on the bed, exhausted by the experience. Thankfully, it was a dream. A terrible dream.

"Are you alright? Your screams scared me to death." Aymelek wore a concerned expression.

Kratos and Aymelek sat down next to me, looking at me curiously, wanting to know what had happened. I tried to release their stress by saying, "Just a bad dream. I am okay." Kratos hugged me.

My screams had attracted Seren from nearby homes. I

found guardians and Seren standing at the door, wondering what had happened. Once they realized everything was okay, they began to disperse. I was still overwhelmed by the magnitude of the shocking experience but started to think about what it meant; Was it just a bad dream, or was it something more than that.

Then, I told Aymelek and Kratos what I had experienced. They were very disturbed by it. Aymelek thought it was more than a dream. A vision. We discussed it at length and reached the conclusion that there was a good chance that if the wizard tried to take the power of the Moontree, he would die. But it was just that—a possibility. The dream could have been just a dream. We couldn't really take the risk. We had to stop the wizard from trying it.

We went to the healer's home when the night ended and met the elders there. After recounting my conversation with the wizard, I told them about my dream. They were stunned.

Jinyan asked Alev, "Do you believe the Moontree can kill the wizard? If so, all we need to do is wait for him to try and do it."

"Who knows? It might. But then, it might not be able to do that. We can't risk it. We have to stop him no matter what." Alev spoke forcefully.

"But how?" Aymelek said. "He is a powerful wizard. We have no means to fight him. And we know that today or tomorrow, he will be here to get what he wants. It's not like we can just talk him out of it. After all, we don't matter to him. The Moontree, the land, Seren—he doesn't care for anything but his assumed mission." It seemed that Aymelek had already given up. But I had an idea. I didn't know if it could work, but it was better than nothing.

"I think that is exactly what we should do: talk him out of it. If we could convince him that attacking the Moontree could cost him his life, he might change his mind."

"You want to tell him about the Moontree? Why don't we present it on a platter to him?" Jinyan was baffled by my idea.

Alev said, "Calm down, Jinyan. No one is doing that. We know very well that the wizard will come for the Moontree sooner or later."

"Alright. But why would the wizard believe him?" Jinyan challenged.

Alev replied, "We have to take a risk since there is nothing else to try."

After the midday meal, I left to find the wizard.

Chapter 15

Kratos was not happy with the prospect of my meeting with the wizard alone and insisted on coming with me. He suggested that we take some guardians along. They could hide in the forest and protect me if needed, but I refused. I believed that if the wizard discovered them, he might become aggressive. Kratos protested but had to give in in the end. Still, he came with me to the village border. He wanted to wait there till I came back. I felt his worried eyes on me till I disappeared into the deep forest.

Qilam and the wizard were nowhere to be found. I looked for them for a long time and eventually found the wizard far away from the village. He was sitting on a rock, deep in thought. I cleared my throat loudly to get his attention. He was surprised to see me but greeted me cheerfully, "Welcome, Thinker! What brings you so far from the village?"

Without wasting time on pleasant conversation, I decided to come right to the purpose of the meeting. "I came to talk to you about an important matter. I know why you are still here. You want to collect as much power as possible before you go."

"Yes, I have told you this myself. What's new about that?"

"First, tell me: how much power can your body take? There has to be a limit."

The wizard frowned and said thoughtfully, "I don't know that."

I was happy with his answer. I asked my next question, "Do you know what will happen if you try to take energy from something that has far more power than you can manage?"

He was clearly uneasy. "No, I don't know that either. Why are you asking this?"

"I had a dream last night. It felt more like a sign. I saw you taking power from the most powerful source on the island—the Moontree."

His eyes twinkled at the mention of the Moontree, "So, that's what it is. The Moontree!"

"Yes. The Moontree is the most powerful living thing on this island."

"So, what happened when I took its energy?" he asked excitedly.

He expected an encouraging answer, but I disappointed him, "You died."

"What? I died? How is that possible? Oh, it was just a dream. And dreams are just that—dreams." He was quite visibly shocked by my answer but tried to shrug it off.

"Yes, it might be just a dream, but what if there really is a limit? What would happen if you exceeded that? If you ask me, it seems quite probable that you would be affected badly."

He paced around in deep thought. Then, he stopped to look at me, frowning. "How do I know if you really had a dream? How do I know you are not playing me? You are trying to protect your precious trees. I remember very well how emotional you were about that tree yesterday."

"Yes, you are right. I don't want anyone to hurt the trees. They are too important for the survival of the island. I know it doesn't matter to you whether the island lives or not, but I want you to take my warning seriously. I am not trying to deceive you. I saw what I saw. And I believe this is exactly what would happen if you try to hurt the Moontree."

I could see that my words had put the seeds of doubt in his mind. Everything was going as I wanted. But the next step was difficult. I didn't know if he would agree to that.

He stayed silent for a moment before he asked the question I was waiting for. "If you are not lying and actually saw this dream, there could be a possibility that it is dangerous for me. But, a far more likely explanation is that you are just telling a lie, trying to protect the island."

I smiled. I already had my answer ready. "I can prove that I am not lying. You can read my mind."

He was both surprised and curious at the same time. He did not know about this power and wanted to learn how to do it. I told him about Alia and her ability to reflect a person's feelings so that everyone around could experience them and how it was used to find out if a person was lying or telling the truth.

"You can experience my feelings as your own. If you agree, I can talk to the elders. I will inform you when they are convinced, and you can come to the village."

"And you will just volunteer to expose your inner thoughts in front of everyone?"

"Yes, if it results in saving the island, then yes, I will," I responded in a confident voice.

"Hmm, you do realize that you can't fight me? I will not tolerate any tricks or deception." His words were cold.

"I know, and I have no such intention."

"Alright then. Let's go to the village right now and be done with it." He started to walk toward the village.

I pretended that I was not prepared for that. "Wait, I told you I will have to talk to the elders first."

"There is no need for that. They will agree to it whether they like it or not. And since you are telling the truth, there is nothing to worry about, right?" He sounded amused. Without waiting for an answer, he walked on.

I walked back to the village with excitement. The conversation had gone exactly the way I had hoped.

I was sure Aymelek would have told the elders about my idea. I had only shared it with her before coming to meet the wizard. I couldn't tell Kratos as I was afraid he might not agree to it.

Kratos was waiting for me. He was not expecting the wizard,

of course. "What is he doing here?" he asked me. The wizard ignored him and kept walking.

I tried to calm him down. "It's alright, Kratos. Everything is fine. Come with me." He was not happy and walked along in a grumpy mood.

The elders were shocked to see the wizard coming with me so casually. Aymelek had told them about my plan, but they didn't expect it to work so easily.

Still, they were already present near the Moontree along with Boris, Idir, and many others. The wizard walked directly to the Moontree and assessed it. We held our breath. The images from my dreams haunted me. Was I wrong in bringing him here? Panic built up inside me.

The wizard studied the Moontree for some time, then he turned to me and said, "Shall we start?"

I was relieved. Aymelek quickly helped Alia with what she needed. When everything was ready, I sat down, facing her. A vial of Moonlight was on the ground in the middle. A Moonflower was floating around slowly. Alia asked me to put my hands on the vial. I placed my hands on it.

The wizard moved closer to watch.

Alia remained quiet for some time with her eyes closed, her hands resting over the glowing light. I had seen it before and knew that she was channeling her energy through the Moonlight, getting ready to test me.

The soft, cool glow spread over my hands, taking them under its dominance. Its coolness spread further instantly.

I felt the cool Moonlight circulating throughout my body. Alia put her hands over mine and held them gently. Something reached my mind. I shuddered at the alien touch and tried to move away from it, but the strange presence was mighty. I couldn't fight it off while it started to probe my mind relentlessly. An array of emotions ran through me, and the alien probe went out of focus, though I could still feel it.

I looked at the Tree Circle. The trees looked beautiful—majestic, in fact. Even sacred. Serenus itself was majestic. I felt happy to be here. A white flame danced in front of my eyes as I looked around. It was coming out of my hands. I watched it, cherishing its unearthly beauty.

I looked up and saw Kratos standing quietly, looking back at me. I felt an immense amount of affection toward him. He was much more than a friend. Even the thought of losing him was unbearable for me. I wished I could stay with him forever.

Tears ran down my cheeks as my attention drifted to the image of Feray sitting broken and desolate in her prison room, waiting for her fate.

Then I looked at Aymelek. It made me sad. She had lost Alfred, her best friend, and was deceived by Feray, her teacher. Her work and the Light-trees were constantly under attack. She did not deserve this stress. If only I could take her sadness away.

Next, I looked at the elders. My head bowed in respect. They were battling one problem after another. It was not an easy life, and their old shoulders were laden with the weight of responsibility. I felt sorry for them.

Finally, I looked at the wizard and felt pity for him. No one cared for him. There were no friends in his life, and he didn't even understand what it meant to care for someone. The image changed in my head, and I saw him standing near the Moontree. Fear ran through me as he walked toward it. I felt helpless as I watched him draining the life out of the Moontree, worrying that at any moment, the Moontree would wither, and with that, Serenus would become a place of misery. But then, something unexpected happened. The power of the Moontree was too much for the wizard to take. His screams echoed around me. In blinding Moonlight, the wizard's body burst. A strong emotion of pity came back and hovered around for a bit, but then my mind went dark.

Something brushed past my mind, waking me up again. It was the same alien presence I had sensed before. It went through my mind looking for something. I wondered what it was that it wanted. The search became intense and insisting.

I heard Alia's frustrated voice. "What are you hiding from me?"

The white flame erupted into the furious red fire as the presence went through my head, and Alia's voice echoed in my mind.

"How? How are you doing this?"

I snapped out of the trance and saw Alia looking at me with angry eyes. She said through clenched teeth, "What is it that you are hiding from me? And how? Tell me everything you know."

"I have no idea what you are talking about," I replied.

"I'll warn you, do not lie. Tell me what you know."

She kept insisting that there was something that I was keeping from her, somehow. She didn't make sense. I told her again that I didn't know what she asked, but she wouldn't listen.

She clenched my hands and closed her eyes. The flame rose higher as her anger seemed to fuel it. The alien presence was back in my head, looking around, searching for what she wanted to know. The glow around her grew more prominent and angrier. It spread around and soon took over the entire place, engulfing us. The Light trees around us became invisible behind the glow, and now it was just the two of us inside an ever-spreading bubble of fiery fog, sitting in front of each other, her hands tightening the grip over mine, hurting my fingers in frustration. The stranger in my head enhanced its energy. I felt its power increase and take control.

I was too weak to fight back. The power insisted that I hand over the information I had kept safe, but I had nothing to give. It was confused and desperate at not being able to unlock the hidden information. It left me once again.

"Tell me what you know. Tell me how you are keeping it from me." Her words were accompanied by a wave of raw anger.

The fire burned higher and higher. My refusal to accept that I knew something further infuriated her. She yelled at me, clenching my hands in frustration.

"You have met your creator, and you are your child. How?"

I grimaced as her nails dug into my skin. I told her I didn't know what she was talking about. It made no sense to me, but her anger and frustration continued to soar. I tried to think about what she may be talking about but failed to find anything to match her claim. I frowned. "Creator? Child? What are you talking about? What is wrong with you?"

She responded with yet another attack on my mind. This time, she was brutal, inconsiderate of the pain her presence brought along. My mind throbbed with every attempt she made. The flames burned vigorously, and an uncomfortable heat spread around us. I started to sweat as it suffocated me. I was sure that I would fall unconscious any moment now.

The flame swayed in front of my eyes, then, suddenly, my senses became sharp and alert again. I felt outraged. I was angry at being unable to get past the invisible wall in the mind that I was searching for. I needed that information at any price. I growled with frustration when every attempt seemed to return unsuccessful. I needed more power, perhaps. But would I be able to deal with so much Moonlight? I didn't know.

Out of frustration, I changed my technique. Now, I was looking for the truth. The mind was innocent and confused. I studied it intensely but realized with surprise that it believed that it knew nothing else. It wasn't trying to hide anything, yet I could feel another power inside it that was far beyond my reach, not letting me access what I needed to know. I was not going to give in so easily. I explored the mind with every ounce of energy I had for a long time. Gradually, the struggle drained me, leaving me weak and helpless. Keeping up the search was futile. I was powerless in the face of the stubborn force that seemed to mock my inability to even compete with it. Finally, I gave up and slumped down, tired and exhausted.

Kratos's voice pulled me out of the alien place I was stuck in. The light trees came back into view. I was lying on the ground with Kratos bent over me with worry etched on his face. The mysterious glow was gone. I looked toward Alia to find her on the ground, being helped by Boris. Her anger had finally withered away.

The wizard was watching me intently.

Many Seren men and women were gathered around us. One of them asked, "What was all this about? What happened to you, Alia? This is not you. I couldn't even recognize the person you transformed into. What is it you are looking for?" His voice was urgent and strict.

Boris helped Alia sit up. She was breathing heavily with a drawn face. Her calm composure had shattered to reveal a side that was unrecognizable even by her friends.

She took some time to catch her breath and then replied weakly, "This mind carries information but doesn't give it away. It stays locked. There is a power inside it that I have never felt before. I did all I could, but I didn't get it." Then she added, looking at me furiously, "I need that information!"

To her, nothing else seemed to matter now, not even what everyone thought of her desperate attempts.

By then, Kratos had helped me get up. A Seren brought me

some water. I felt better but was still shocked by the strange experience. When I was about to fall unconscious, I realized that my mind had started feeling the emotions Alia the Mirror was going through. The intensity of her desire to know about whatever she thought I was hiding surprised me. I was not sure about her claim, though. I didn't have any powers to hide anything from her. But she not only believed in her claim but also tried her utmost to find out about it.

Alia's inability to find what was hidden in my mind puzzled everyone. They knew something was there, which was more capable than Alia could handle.

The wizard had stood away silently throughout the incident, watching and feeling everything. Now, he left his place and walked toward me. "Come, Thinker! We need to talk."

Chapter 16

I wandered in the yard, leaving footprints in the fresh snow. I opened my hand to let the soft snowflakes land on my palm. They were light and beautiful and melted away quickly, leaving a wet mark of freshness. It was the first time I had seen snow. And would perhaps be the last.

A gust of wind shook the snow-covered branches of the tree I was passing under. It showered me. I enjoyed the cold that spread around my neck and looked up. The sky was generous, raining down snowflakes in heavy blankets. It looked brighter for the time of the day.

The evening was approaching fast. My last evening here. The thought froze my heart. I looked around and stopped at the Tree Circle. I went closer, enjoying the feel of the fresh snow under my feet. The trees were hidden under the white veil, yet their glow peeked through, giving out hues of different colors. They looked splendid as they stood calm and peaceful among the dancing white. Standing in front of the Tree Circle, I tried to imprint the snow-streaked wonder in my mind. I wanted to capture the image, burn it in my memory, to cherish it forever. I was happy that I had the chance to see this snowy landscape before I left.

Aymelek's voice disturbed my thoughts. I turned around to

see her standing at the front door. She gestured for me to come. I turned away with a last look around and walked back to the healer's home. I brushed the snow off my head and shoulders before going inside. Everyone was there waiting for me. They wanted to know what the wizard talked to me about.

I sat back in my chair and sighed. The time I was dreading was here. I had to tell my friends something that would hurt them. Looking at their faces sadly, I told them, "The wizard wants me to go with him through the Dark End."

Everyone gasped. Kratos took my hand and gripped it tightly. "You are not going anywhere. I won't let you."

His gesture brought tears to my eyes. "I have to go. To save the Moontree. To save Serenus and all of you."

"What are you talking about?" Aymelek said. "Save from who? The wizard felt what you dreamed and left the Moontree alone. There is no problem anymore. He will soon leave us."

"He only left because I agreed to go with him. He was not fully convinced that my dream could come true. He offered me a deal, and I took it."

"But why? What does he want from you?" It was Alev's concerned voice.

"Since he knows about the power that Alia says I have in me, he is curious. He wants to take me with him because he believes I am important somehow. In return, he promised to spare the Moontree and leave the island as soon as tomorrow morning." I paused and then said sadly, "I will leave in the morning with him."

Kratos stood up in anger. "This is not happening. I won't let it. We will find a way to send him alone."

"There *is* no way. He will attack the Moontree if I refuse. And we can't force him to leave."

Kratos was beside himself with sadness. He started to pace in the room as others discussed how to send the wizard alone. Listening to their desperate thoughts was agonizing. I was exhausted by the very idea of tomorrow's sunrise. But sitting here, watching my friends in helpless misery, was unbearable.

"I am tired and want to rest," I muttered.

Everyone fell silent and watched me for a moment. Kratos recovered quickly and said, "Yes, sure. I will take you to the room."

He accompanied me to one of the bedrooms and helped me get the warm blankets. I lay in the bed, snuggling in for warmth.

Kratos sat in front of me and tried to comfort me. "Don't worry. I said I would find a way, and I will. If we can't convince the wizard, we will trick him. But I will not let you go." He closed the door gently behind him.

I spent the evening in bed, watching the snow falling continuously outside the window. The Tree Circle was glowing invitingly. Before it became dark, I left the room to eat my dinner but couldn't stomach much. I could hear everyone's voices, still planning and thinking of ways to stop the wizard from taking me with him. I was proud of them for not giving up even though I had made up my mind.

I needed fresh air, and in the hope of finding some peace, I left the healer's home and walked to the Greentree. Inside its chamber, I thought about all the unanswered questions. Why did I come here? Was it right to leave? Who sent me, and why did they give me a poem? I had tried before, but even the wisdom of the tree couldn't provide me with these answers. I decided to think about a way to stop the wizard. I felt like I was leaving the island too early. I could have done so much more and thought about many other things. As the Greenlight took effect, I sat under its glow and became lost in my thoughts, in a conversation with myself or the tree. Whatever it was. I still wasn't sure how it worked.

After some time, I returned to the chamber, still without any answers. But I had found a new perspective. A new way of reading the poem, and it gave me hope. There was no way to know if it was correct, but I had to share it with others.

I walked back toward the healer's home and thought about telling them. It was a sensitive matter. I had to convey it cautiously, ensuring that they understood it could be wrong.

As I walked through the entrance, everyone turned to me with hopeful eyes, expecting a solution to the problem, but I had none. I shook my head. Their faces changed to reflect the sadness as they, too, had failed to come up with any plans. I went back to the bedroom, and once again, they became busy in whispers.

I thought about the appropriate words to tell everyone about the poem, and when I was satisfied with the wording, I found some papers and wrote down my newfound understanding. I made several copies. Each addressed one of my friends and elders. I used the opportunity to thank them for their kindness and wrote what their companionship meant to me.

Aymelek's notebook was sitting on the table. I picked it up to hide the messages in it. I wanted them to find it after I was gone. I left the pages in the notebook and walked to the window to look out in the dark and enjoy the sight of the glowing trees for the last time.

Aymelek came through the open door and stood by me. For some time, we stayed quiet, just looking through the window with empty eyes. Then she spoke, "I don't know what will happen tomorrow. But there is something I want you to read." She handed me a page. "Alfred left this for me before going into the dark. I want you to know." She added soberly.

Surprised by her words, I took the page, and started to read.

In a mysterious world,

I opened my eyes,

Curious and frightened,

I looked left and right.

A dream, an instinct,

A poem in my heart.

And what's on my wrist?

A very strange watch.

I don't know from where,

And why I have come.

Few threads to follow,

And clues only some!

The past is lost,

Nothing comes to mind.

Others came before me,

And tried to find.

Don't get me wrong,

They're really kind,

But their failure to answer,

Has kept us behind.

At every big question,

We've nothing to show,

Shake our heads, we say,

We do not know.

Will I be different,

Or, like others, stay blind?

To pull on the right thread,

To unravel and unwind,

I'll need to think,

Outside the box.

Because what I seek,

Many have sought.

If I am to succeed,

Find something but naught,

What would I need?

Where should I start?

An untried action,

Not a battle we've fought,

An all-new direction,

A new line of thought!

To find common ground,

An understanding profound,

I started by looking,

Observing and learning.

I'm writing it all,

Whatever I have found,

Questions and lessons,

From all around.

Who made this world?

Why and for what?

A child at play,

Or an engineer at work?

We've theories and opinions,

And numerous guesses.

Our stories sow divisions,

And disastrous messes!

Not bringing us together,

They keep us divided.

Imagine finding a tether,

That's not one-sided;

A belief beyond doubt,

To finally bring about;

A beacon of hope,

That's not lopsided.

I've heard the rumors,

And hoped against hope,

They tell me I'll find it,

In the lost scroll!

An idea, a message,

A beautiful goal,

The real deal,

No tricks,

No lump of coal.

To unite us where needed,

But allow our differences.

Leave room for possibilities,

But erase all distances.

Wholesome and wise conduct,

For a world exquisite!

Where goodness is a product,

Not pre-requisite.

The idea of an open mind,

Not vengeful and punishing,

Accepting all and being kind,

Beautiful and ravishing!

If such a scroll exists indeed,

Trying to find it-a worthy deed.

No way to guess if I will succeed,

Wish me the best and god-speed.

Everything,

But you,

I'm putting on the line.

What else can I give,

I hope I'll be fine.

I believe in myself,

I'll find the scroll.

Study every bookshelf,

Defeat every troll.

Then,

Together we will stand,

On the other side,

With the scroll in my hand,

But no fear and no pride.

But if all goes bad,

And we never see again.

Do not be sad,

And feel no pain.

Remember the memories,

And times spent together.

No-one can steal it,

It's ours forever.

In every new comer,

Of white or black Color,

In pursuit of the secret,

As John or as Egrett,

In their longing,

And their passion,

Whether a he or a she,

You will always find me.

I will be missing you until we meet again.

-Alfred.

I couldn't help but feel impressed by the Seren I had never met. Aymelek was still looking outside with a blank expression. I reread the poem. Now I had a much better understanding of why Alfred left.

I handed the poem to Aymelek but couldn't say any words. She took the page, patted on my shoulder, and left the room. I went to bed thinking about Alfred's words.

* * *

On my last day in Serenus, we walked to the Dark End in the form of a procession. Every Seren had come to say goodbye, many of them with teary eyes. They knew that I was leaving Serenus so that the Moontree could be safe from the power-thirsty wizard. Their open display of gratitude and love melted my heart. They brought small tokens of their love and respect to take with me. It was hard to refuse them, but I couldn't leave with so much when I didn't even know if I was going to a new world or to my death. The only thing that I was taking with me was the pendant from Kratos. He had given it to me during our stay at the Serenus Lodge. I couldn't bear to part with it.

The wizard and Qilam were waiting for us at the shore. As we approached them, Qilam ran over to me and said excitedly, "I wasn't sure you would come. Remember, I said I would do what I believe in? Your words convinced me to take the leap of faith. I am going with you." I frowned at him and looked away. I didn't care if he thought my words were responsible for his decision.

Qilam and the wizard were leaving in a boat each, but there was also a third boat full of supplies. Qilam explained, "Just in case the journey is long."

Saying goodbye to Idir, Fabio, and Misa was hard. I whispered to them to take care of Kratos for me. They nodded and promised they wouldn't leave him alone.

Pari gave me a beautiful round stone and stood by soberly. I thanked her for the gift.

Then I turned toward Aymelek. The moment our eyes met, she broke into tears. I stood there, hugging her without saying a word. She sobbed openly. Then, she took off her ring. It was the ring that had mesmerized me with its unique beauty the first time I saw it. A white translucent sphere with wispy White Light was swirling slowly inside. She handed it to me and said, "This sphere has the first Moonlight ever captured. It has been worn solely by the healers chosen by it. If it likes a healer, it keeps swirling. If not, the light stays still. It is believed that it is the most powerful Moonlight as it was taken directly from the Moontree bulb the moment it was born. I want you to have it."

I hesitated but eventually agreed. I understood how precious this ring was for her. I thanked her, and she hugged me again. It was becoming even harder to leave.

"Come on, Thinker! It's time to go," the wizard said impatiently. He was getting irritated by the emotional environment around him.

Finally, Idir gently held her arm. "Aymelek, let's not send our friend away with tears." He gave her a meaningful look.

She nodded and tried to compose herself. "I know, it is just that… what if?" With one last hug, she moved away.

Kratos stood next to my boat as the guardians brought it and placed it in the water. Boris put a bag inside it and said, "Just some food for the journey." He moved forward, hugged me quickly, and then left.

The elders' torn faces revealed their disdain for what was happening, but they couldn't do anything. I hugged them, and they moved back.

"Thinker, be done with it now." The wizard had tolerated enough.

Kratos was the last Seren I needed to say goodbye to. I wasn't ready to say the words yet. I looked at his face and stood there, frozen. I didn't know what to say. There were no words that could tell any of my friends what I felt for them and how sad I was at leaving them, but also how lucky I felt that I had met them and spent time with them.

Kratos moved forward and hugged me tightly, whispering

in my ear, "Don't worry. Just remember what I told you."

I was confused. What did Kratos mean by that? Was he going to do something to fight the wizard? A worry popped its head inside me.

Everyone else had already stepped back. Unwillingly, Aymelek, Idir, and Kratos stepped back a few steps.

Boris and two guardians carried a rather large bag and awkwardly passed by me to place it in the boat. Boris spoke sheepishly, "We don't know how long the journey could be."

The wizard was looking at the Dark End, ready to go. He didn't want to wait any longer and came close to Qilam and me and said, "If we leave early, we might reach the next island in daylight. Let's go!"

Boris stepped forward and, to everyone's surprise, punched Qilam in the face. He screamed in pain as he fell back and started cursing him. Boris moved back.

The wizard looked at Qilam and smiled. "What a farewell you have earned, Qilam."

The guardians looked at me and nodded, then they moved toward the wizard and said, "If you want to leave, you can go. No one else is leaving." Something was happening. I looked at them, trying to understand what they were doing.

The wizard turned furious, "What are you trying to do? You know I am too powerful for you. Why do you want to waste your life?"

I saw Kratos and Boris go behind the wizard, surrounding

him. I looked at Kratos with questioning eyes. What was he going to do? He couldn't possibly fight the wizard. And I did not want anyone to get hurt.

As soon as the wizard realized that he was encircled, he spread his arms dangerously, facing the nearby guardian. He strained his muscles like he did on the island under the fall. I was sure he would attack the guardian with a spell. I wanted them to stop wasting their lives in a futile effort and yelled, "Stop this! No one has to suffer. I made a deal with him. I will honor that deal. Step back."

The wizard waited for just a second for the guardians to move back, but they didn't.

"Alright then, that's enough!" He waved his arm, but nothing happened. In shock, he looked at his hands and tried again. Still nothing.

Kratos exclaimed, "It works!" The wizard turned around and faced him and tried the spell on him, but to his dismay, nothing happened.

I was as stumped as the wizard. How were they stopping him from using magic?

Boris and the guardians pounced on him before he could fly away to escape the uncertain situation. Kratos and Idir held on as guardians opened the large bag from my boat and pulled out a rope. They used the rope to tie up the struggling wizard.

I heard the entire village sigh in relief as they understood what was happening. Still not knowing how, I stood there, watching with a mystified look.

The wizard was yelling commands at us, and behind him, Qilam was still on the ground, watching in disbelief.

Idir spoke to address my confusion, "Apparently, you are not the only thinker here. Sometimes, we can think too." He laughed as he teased me, withholding the information that I sought.

Guardians put Qilam in his boat, and he was the first one to be sent forward. He screamed in panic. Everyone knew he was a coward, but no one expected such a show of wailing from him after he was already ready to go. As he disappeared into the dark, the screaming stopped. Even the wizard was surprised at hearing his screams.

Boris said mockingly, "Wasn't he ready to go a few moments ago?"

Then, the guardians carried the wizard to his boat and pushed it into the water. Before he disappeared, he yelled more threats, "I will come back, and I will burn this entire world to the ground. You will all pay for this." We stood watching him as he disappeared into the dark.

Idir and Kratos stood teasingly in front of me as more Seren ran over. I looked back at them, but they wouldn't tell me how they had pulled this off. I understood what they meant. It was a challenge for me to figure out.

I scratched my head, then put my hand on my chin as my friends watched me with mischievous smiles. I felt embarrassed at not being able to come up with an explanation for how they stopped the wizard's magic from affecting them.

Fabio and Misa also didn't know. They begged for answers, but Idir shook his head.

Kratos said, "This is for the thinker to think."

I looked at Aymelek with pleading eyes. She smiled and shook her head, but for a moment, I sensed sadness in her eyes. She laughed, and I realized that it was nothing. I brought my attention back to the waiting faces in front of me, teasing me to crack the puzzle.

Finally, I gave up and said, "Okay, I cannot wait anymore. I need to know. Don't make me go sit under the Greentree. At least give me a hint."

Idir looked at Kratos, who nodded.

"What do the seven Lighttrees do when the Moontree runs out of light?" Idir asked.

Still confused, I replied, "They become dangerous and steal life from things around them to refill the bulb in the Moontree."

Idir teased, "And what was this wizard's ability?"

My jaw dropped as I realized how simple the answer was. I laughed at their clever trick and said, "He did the same as the seven. We just needed some Moonlight to stop him from being dangerous."

Kratos pulled out a locket from under his shirt. He was wearing the tiny Moonlight vial that Feray used to wear and was able to go in and out of the tree under the fall. Idir, Boris, and the guardians had Moonlight vials in their pockets.

Fabio and Misa were still thinking with open mouths when Idir finally explained it to them, "The wizard could not hurt anyone with Moonlight. That is why, in the dream, he was killed by Moontree. Just like the seven trees, we stopped him from harming us by carrying Moonlight vials on us."

Kratos added, "And when he couldn't use magic, he was just an ordinary Seren."

Fabio was nodding excitedly. He understood it now. "He came only two nights before a full moon, but the night was cloudy..."

Misa interrupted and completed the joke, "Poor wizard. Just needed some Moonlight in his life."

We laughed and thoroughly enjoyed their clever remarks.

By now, a whole crowd had gathered around us. I looked to my right and spotted Alev smiling proudly at Idir and Kratos. Then, she asked, "And if the thinker couldn't figure this out, who did?"

Idir replied, "Last night, we were trying to find a way to trick the wizard. We were thinking out loud, saying many ideas, when Kratos said the wizard is able to steal the life out of the living things. Then Aymelek said, just like the seven trees do without the Moonlight. Then I said: How do we stop his ability? What could be his weakness? And Kratos said, just like the seven trees? And then we screamed the answer together—the Moonlight!"

The elders and the Seren surrounding us laughed heartily and shook their heads. Alev held my hand. I looked at her. She nodded her head once. I nodded back, remembering how she had greeted me the day I had arrived on the island, with the nod of the head and raise of a glass. She said teasingly, "Picked a name yet?" Everyone laughed again.

I looked at the happy faces of my friends all around me, still not believing that we had prevailed against a powerful wizard once again. Eventually, we started to head back to the village. The rest of the Seren had already left, relieved that the threat of an attack was over.

"Don't you think the situation demands a celebration? Let's go to the village center and celebrate," Fabio suggested. Everyone agreed, and we began to walk away toward the village.

A loud splash made our heads turn. We froze as we saw Aymelek pushing a boat toward the Dark End. She had gone to pick up my bag from the boat. I was so happy in the excitement of our success that I didn't see her push it into the water. Everyone gasped as we watched her get in the boat and head toward the dark barrier. We ran to her, but she was already in the current.

She looked back at us and said, "I will miss you and never forget you. I hope you can forgive me, but Alfred is waiting for me. I can't live here when he is all alone, waiting for me there."

We screamed at the top of our lungs as we tried to convince her to stop, even though it was too late. She kept looking at us sadly while we ran after her in the water, but Boris and guardians held us back, and we watched her disappear into the dark.

No one could believe what had just happened. We began

mourning her loss. Alev wept loudly, and Boris tried to comfort her. Kratos was on his knees, looking into the dark with a frozen face. I put my hand on his shoulder, and at the same time, Idir put his hand on the other shoulder. I looked at Idir. I was thankful that he was there to be with Kratos.

I wept uncontrollably as I realized that I had failed Aymelek. She was sad, and I could not make her feel better. Even a few moments ago, I had sensed her sadness but then became distracted by the celebration. Then, I remembered the question I had asked her when we were talking about Alfred.

"If you could say one more thing to him, what would it be?"

"Don't leave, but if you must, take me with you."

The image of a sad Aymelek flashed in my head. She was sitting under the Yellowtree, talking about going to the next world. I had assumed it was just the tree that was affecting her thoughts, but I had promised her, *If we ever leave, we will leave together.*

I didn't know where she was going. There was no way of knowing if she would have to face Esmeray, Qilam, and the wizard in the next world and whether she would be able to find Alfred all by herself. I thought about what she might have to go through. And, of course, the biggest question was whether there actually was a next world to go to.

I looked at the ring she left me with. She had given it to me to protect me against the wizard, but now she was without protection. *If we ever leave, we will leave together.* I repeated my promise in my head.

I knew I wasn't ready, but I had to go after her. I waited for an opportunity and then ran to the last empty boat and pushed it into the water as my friends screamed for me to stop and ran after me. Before they could reach me, I, too, was leaving them forever. I sat facing the people I loved and was hurting.

"I am so sorry!" I shouted. "I promised Aymelek that I would go with her if she went into the dark."

Kratos fell down, Alev ordered me to return, Boris and guardians ran one more time but once again, it was too late. I looked at Idir. He was sitting next to Kratos, examining him. Then, he looked up at me and nodded. I knew what he meant. Kratos would be okay.

I was going into the dark, but the darkness seemed to be moving ahead too. My boat traveled toward it, but it kept its distance and moved ahead. I looked at my friends one last time. They stared back in disbelief and shock. Our eyes remained locked until they disappeared out of sight.

Then, I faced forward. There was no sign of any other boat in front of me. Just an endless dark fog that was becoming lighter as I approached it. The veil surrounded me on all sides as I traveled forward to an unknown destination inside a bubble of light.

I looked around to see if I could spot anything in the dark. As my boat passed it, a dead fish floated on the surface of the water. Then another one—no, this one wasn't a fish, it was something else, and it was too far to recognize what it was. My heart started racing, and fear took over me.

Gradually, the fog started to become thicker, and the circle of light surrounding me began to shrink. I sat helpless as the darkness covered me. I could no longer see anything. I felt it drain all energy out of my body, and I fell backward.

As long as I could, I resisted and fought the dark, trying to stay awake, but as it sucked all light out of me, I fell asleep.

The End.

About The Author

nalid Ejaz is a software engineer by profession and blessed a thinking mind. The Lost Scroll is his brainchild. He loves create fantasy worlds to present complex philosophical concepts in easy-to-understand stories. His writing style generates thought-provoking content that interests a younger audience as much as it attracts adults.

About The Co-Author

Tahira Ejaz is the co-author of Serenus. The first book in The Lost Scroll series. She lives with her husband and four boys and is in love with nature. Her romance is reflected in everything she does, from crocheting, knitting, gardening, paper making, and interior designing to story writing.

She holds the degree of Master of Science in Applied Psychology and Master of Arts in English Language and Literature. She works as a curriculum advisor for a private school.

Reach us at:
Instagram: https://www.instagram.com/factandlore/
Email: info@factandlore.com

Made in United States
North Haven, CT
11 May 2022